Storylandia

The Wapshott Journal
of Fiction

Issue 19

The Wapshott Press

Storylandia, Issue 19, The Wapshott Journal of Fiction, ISSN 1947-5349, ISBN 978-1-942007-10-4, is published at intervals by the Wapshott Press, now a 501(c)(3) nonprofit, PO Box 31513, Los Angeles, California, 90031-0513, telephone 323-201-7147. All correspondence can be sent The Wapshott Press, PO Box 31513, LA CA 90031-0513. Visit our website at www.WapshottPress.org to learn more. This work is copyright © 2016 by Storylandia. The Wapshott Journal of Fiction, Los Angeles, California. Copyright © 2016 Kathryn L. Ramage and is reprinted here with the copyright owner's permission. Copyright for the cover artwork is held by Kathryn L. Ramage, and is used here with her permission.

Storylandia is always seeking quality original short stories, novelettes, and novellas. Please have a look at our submission guidelines at www.Storylandia.WapshottPress.org or email the editor at editor@wapshottpress.org

Many thanks to editor William Akin for the proofread and editorial support.

Cover: "Ghost of a Tower," by Kathryn L. Ramage

Storylandia

The Wapshott Journal of Fiction

Founded in 2009

Issue 19, Autumn 2016

Edited by Ginger Mayerson

Table of Contents

Who Killed Toby Glovins?

By Kathryn L. Ramage

Who Killed Toby Glovins?

1

The marriage of Miss Amelia Marsh to Evelyn Tollarhithe was a long-anticipated event. The two had been sweethearts from childhood, and their respective families believed that it was only a matter of time before the courtship came to a satisfactory conclusion. After the double tragedy at Marsh Hall that spring, Amelia left her home to stay with Evelyn's family at Foxgrove, Sir Percival Tollarhithe's estate near Norwich. The wedding was announced for September. As the eventful day drew near, friends and relatives made plans to attend.

Two days before the wedding, Amelia's cousins Frederick Babington and the Honourable Captain Kellynch Marsh drove from Freddie's flat in London with Sir Percival's son, Phillip. From there, the journey normally took two or three hours, but Phillip and Kell insisted on stopping frequently along the way.

"You don't have to come if you don't want to," Freddie told them at the Green Man Inn. They were barely five miles from the gates of Foxgrove Park and might be there within a quarter-hour—if only his cousins would *move*. Phillip and Kell, however, seemed content to sit in the bar-parlor. "If you'll let me have the roadster, Kell, I'll drive on by myself. You two can sit here for the rest of the afternoon, then take a train back to London. Better to turn back than drag your feet every step of the way."

"I couldn't turn back if I wanted to," said Phil. "I've been summoned. Mother wrote me last week to ask if I were coming home for this wedding—and when Mother 'asks' in that particular way, I'm not allowed to say No."

"I'll come." Kell sighed and sat forward to put his empty glass down on the table. "I promised Mellie I would, and I won't disappoint her. Besides, I can't leave Phil to face the wolves alone. It's going to be beastly for both of us with all the Tollarhithes there and most of the Marshes too. An alliance between our two families is a cause for celebration, except in *our* case." He lay his hand on Phillip's arm. "You know how Father feels about us, and I've no choice but to talk to him sooner or later about this air service plan of mine."

"You've faced worse things than your parents, Kell." Kellynch Marsh was in fact a decorated war hero, renowned for his bravery.

"Even facing the whole bally Bosch army doesn't seem so terrible right now. The worst they can do is shoot at you, and you've a sporting chance to shoot back. Those frozen smiles of Aunt Egeria's are more than I can bear."

"At least my father's not so bad," said Phillip. "He's known about us since we were schoolboys and never made much effort to come between us. I suppose he's still hoping that I'll grow out of it. He'd prefer I concentrate on my studies rather than run around playing detective—but that's more on you, Freddie, than Kell."

The loud puttering sound of an engine outside the inn caught their attention. Kell rose from his seat and went to the nearest window. Freddie followed to see what appeared to be an important cavalcade: A silver Rolls Royce was gliding into the parking area escorted by a motorbike with sidecar.

"It looks like a General arriving," he said.

"General, hell," replied Kell. "It's Mother."

The motorbike pulled up beside Kell's red roadster and two young men clambered out. One pointed to the roadster and turned to speak to the occupants of the Royce. Even from a distance, the heads of the three ladies seated within the grand automobile were familiar: the bright, strawberry-gold waves of Kell's mother, Emily, Lady Marshbourne; the graceful upright figure and long, dark plaits of Theresa Marsh, Amelia's mother; and the smaller, plumper form of Matilda Marsh, her head covered by a flowered hat. The two boys were Matilda's sons, Daedelus and Icarus, called Dotty and Bicky by their friends.

"No sign of Father," Kell observed with some relief. "Maybe he isn't coming. It won't be so bad if it's just Mother and the aunties."

"Aunt Emily's always been decent," Phillip agreed. He drained his glass and set it down on the table with a decisive thump. "All right then. Let's go say hello."

The three went out through a side door into the parking area.

"Kell, dear," Emily cried, lowering her window and extending one hand out towards her son. "Dotty said that that must be your motor-car. And Freddie and Phillip are with you? How wonderful! We were so hoping you boys were going to Foxgrove today."

"Didn't you get my last letter?" Kell asked as he leaned in through the window to bestow a quick kiss on his mother's cheek.

"A week ago, but you also wrote that you were developing some important business deal with an American millionaire. I was afraid that might've kept you."

"Larry Martens is no millionaire, but I think his father is." While spending the summer in London with Freddie, Kell had made the acquaintance of an American youth who had also flown in the war. "We're starting up charter flights for shipping goods and passengers across the Channel. We only want an airport. It's simply a matter of choosing a good spot, putting up a hangar, and buying an aeroplane or two. That's partly why I've come. I wanted to talk to Father about giving me a field he's no better use for. Plenty of flat land in Norfolk and the Marshes own so much of it. Where is he, by the way?"

"Your father? He might not be able to attend. This Mr. Martens, is he a new... friend?" Emily asked delicately and glanced at Phillip.

Kell understood and grinned. "Nothing of the sort. It's purely a business venture. Larry's pining for a girl he left behind in the States and wants to make good before he goes home to pop the question."

This answer seemed to relieve Emily. She was eager to hear more about her son's plans, until the other ladies gently reminded her that they ought to be going if they wanted to reach Foxgrove by teatime. The Royce drove on and the young men returned to their own vehicles to follow it. They were soon at the tall iron gates of Foxgrove Park.

As they proceeded up the long avenue of lime trees, the octagonal Jacobean towers of the house could be glimpsed ahead. The drive opened out into a great circle and the façade of Foxgrove stood before them, a vast red brick wall crisscrossed with a diamond pattern of pale yellow and innumerable mullioned windows framed in stone. The butler and a well-ordered row of footmen stood near the open front door, and with them were Sir Percival and Lady Egeria Tollarhithe. They were a handsome couple: Sir Percival was a distinguished-looking man of 54 with ginger hair turning gray at the temples. His wife was taller than he, with dark chestnut hair in tightly crimped waves held back above her ears by golden combs.

Although a footman was there to open the passenger door of the Royce, Freddie took his aunt's hand to assist her out. Once she gained the ground, Emily gave him a kiss and said, "How well you look, dear boy. So much better than when I saw you last. You haven't brought along that lad who looks after you?"

"No, Aunt Emily. I'm doing much better and don't need Billy to play nurse to me. Besides, there isn't room for four in the roadster. I've given him a week's holiday." At Freddie's suggestion, his manservant Billy Watkins had gone to the village of Abbotshill to see his sweetheart and settle matters between them.

Freddie then assisted the other Marsh ladies. Each in turn kissed his cheek and agreed that he was looking much better than when he'd visited Marsh Hall last spring. His aunts had doted on him since he'd been left orphaned at a young age. Although Emily was most like a mother to him, all three had had a share in his upbringing.

Sir Percival and his lady greeted Emily first, not only as the highest-ranked personage among their guests as the Viscountess Marshbourne, but also Percival's younger sister. Even though Freddie accompanied his aunts, Sir Percival and Lady Egeria paid their respects to Theresa and Matilda before turning their attention to him.

"Frederick, how good of you to come." Egeria took both his hands and bestowed a rather formal kiss. Percival patted his shoulder, shook his hand, and added his own welcome. "And Kellynch." The lady smiled stiffly as Kell came forward. "Welcome to Foxgrove."

"Didn't Phillip come with you boys? Ah, there he is." Percival found his son by the back of the Royce, helping Dotty and Bicky unstrap the luggage. "Never mind that, lads!" he called out to them. "The footmen will take care of the bags." At a gesture from the butler, the footmen hastened to do so. "Come inside."

"Yes, please come in, all of you," added Egeria. "We hoped you'd arrive in time for tea. Much of the family is already here. They'll be so pleased to see you."

She guided her guests to the drawing room, which was crowded with members of the Tollarhithe family: The bridegroom Evelyn and his elder brother Reginald stood with their father Aubrey. The left sleeve of Reginald's coat was pinned shut, for he'd lost his arm below the elbow at the Somme. Evelyn was a boyish-looking youth with sleek, auburn hair and a reddish wisp of mustache; he was generally considered good-looking, but not as handsome as his cousin Felix.

Felix Tollarhithe was Sir Percival's third cousin once removed, and called the baronet "Uncle." He and Evelyn had been best friends from childhood. After his elder brothers Frank and Clement were killed within days of each other in the spring of 1918, Felix had joined the army and Evelyn had gone with him.

The two had only just finished their training and were preparing to go to France when the war ended, to the great relief of their families.

Since Felix had an interest in estate management, he'd been living at Foxgrove this summer while he learned the business from Sir Percival. His parents, who lived in a London suburb, had arrived earlier that afternoon for the wedding and were seated with other visiting relatives.

Felix was at the center of the room amid a giggling group of girls, Evelyn's sisters, Alma and Isolde, and Phillip's sisters, Perdita and Iphigenia, called "Piggy" by her family. Perdita was strawberry-curled and looked very like her aunt Emily. Although she wasn't as pretty as Perdita or as clever as their eldest sister Phaedra, there was nothing porcine about Piggy's manners or appearance despite her nickname. Phaedra, who most resembled their mother, sat apart from the others, near one of the garden windows; she and Reginald had married two years ago and had an infant son, Peveril, who'd been brought down from the nursery for this special occasion.

Great-Uncle Archibald, from another branch of the family, sat in a wing-backed chair by the fire conversing with an elegant lady in her fifties.

As the Marshes entered the room, the assembled Tollarhithes welcomed them. The elegant lady rose from her seat to embrace Emily affectionately. This was Diana Montcliffe, Percival's and Emily's elder sister. She was married to a grandee in Cumberland and hadn't visited her old home in more than ten years.

"How wonderful you look," she said to Emily. "So lovely, no different from the young girl who attended me at my own wedding. Theresa and Matilda, my dears, I would know you anywhere."

"I daresay we haven't changed very much, but you won't know our children," said Matilda. "You haven't seen them since they were small. These two are my sons—Daedelus, the eldest, and this is Icarus. This handsome young man is Emily's Kellynch, and this is Freddie Babington."

"Babington?" Diana murmured and regarded Freddie as if she wondered how someone neither a Tollarhithe nor a Marsh could possibly have found his way into their midst.

"Pamela Marsh's son," Emily explained. "You remember."

"Oh, yes. Yes, of course." Diana gave him a warmer smile. "How very much you resemble your mother, poor dear girl." She looked around the room. "Where is Phillip?"

Phillip had come in with the other boys, but after saying hello to his favorite uncle Aubrey, stopped briefly at the tea-table to greet Piggy and Perdita and his cousins, and to grab a scone, before going to see his new nephew. He sat beside Phaedra, practically hiding behind a potted fern. He wasn't avoiding Diana as much as trying to stay out of his parents' sight.

"What about Mellie?" asked Dotty. "Where is she?"

"Over at the Vixen," Alma reported with a giggle. The Vixen was the family's name for the dower house, which sat behind the larger Foxgrove. Since there'd been no dowager in many years, it was currently the home of Aubrey Tollarhithe, Sir Percival's cousin. "She's working on her wedding dress."

"Is something wrong with the dress?" Theresa asked with a note of deep concern.

"Oh, it's not that. One of her father's American

relatives sent some lovely old Valenciennes lace as a wedding present. Amelia thought it would look smashing with the dress, but it isn't the sort of piece she can use for a veil. There wasn't time to consult the dressmaker and she's determined to sew it on herself. She ought to come in soon. She must've heard that loud motor."

Amelia did come in a few minutes later. She was a pretty girl with large brown eyes and brunette curls cut short in the modern style, more rosy-cheeked and certainly much happier than she'd been when Freddie had seen her at Marsh Hall. He felt shy seeing her again, afraid that she blamed him for how his investigation into the death of their cousin Bertram had ended, but when Mellie noticed him, she smiled. "Freddie, how wonderful! I was afraid you wouldn't come."

After embracing her mother and aunts, Amelia went over to Evelyn and, with a whisper and playful tug on his sleeve, drew him aside. Reginald joined his wife and Philip. Great-Uncle Archibald offered Aubrey the chair Diana had vacated, but Aubrey refused it and instead went around to the other side of the tea-table.

"It's been a very long time since we've had so much of the family together," Egeria said to the Marsh ladies. "I'm sorry to see that Cecilia and Marcus didn't come with you."

"Celia didn't feel up to the long drive. She's expecting her baby next month—her first, you know, and I'm afraid she's having a difficult time of it, poor dear," Matilda explained, adding this last in an undertone. "Marcus has stayed with her, though he was kind enough to lend my boys his motorbike."

"What about Father?" Kell asked his mother.

"You said he wasn't coming."

"Your father's been detained on estate business," Emily answered. "He and your Uncle Kellynch hope to arrive for the wedding. You might tell him all about your aeroplanes then."

Freddie met Kell's eyes and gave him an encouraging smile. It wouldn't be so bad if Kell had to be in his father's company for only one day. Phillip, on the other hand, was in the midst of his entire family.

While Lady Egeria was coolly polite to Kell because of his relationship with Phillip, and cool to Freddie because he was Kell's friend, Sir Percival was honestly glad to see them. His elder son Peter had been killed in the war and the deaths of Felix's brothers not long afterwards had also been a hard blow; Freddie thought he was all the more eager to befriend the young men of his family who had survived.

"I know you won't stay for the shooting after we see Ev and Amelia off," Sir Percival told Freddie and Kell after a long story about how diligently Felix had been rearing a brood of pheasant chicks, "but the local hunt meets here just before Christmas. Will you come for that? It's good exercise, no guns going off, and there's a capital line of our black-tailed foxes in the Threescore Oak Wood. The vixens have outdone themselves for kits the last few years."

Kell refrained from quoting Oscar Wilde on the unspeakable pursuing the uneatable and instead said that it sounded like a jolly idea. He hadn't really ridden since the summer of '14. If Phil were home for the holiday, he'd be happy to come and join in. Sir Percival looked pleased, but his lady did not.

"While you're here, you young men might also help with the flower gathering," she said.

"Gathering flowers, Aunt Eg?" echoed Dotty.

"Aren't the caterers bringing them in?"

"They are, but this is a charming old family tradition that we've revived for the occasion. Aubrey discovered it in a journal kept by one of the Tollarhithe daughters."

"Great Aunt Belinda," Aubrey contributed. "In the 18th century, whenever there was a marriage at Foxgrove, the maidens of the village gathered armloads of wildflowers from the countryside to create a sort of bower for the newlywed couple to sit in during the celebrations. They gathered wildflowers for Aunt Belinda's wedding, but the custom was dying out even then. We can't ask the people of Foxborough to do it these days, but when I told Amelia and the girls about it, they were all very keen and so is Felix."

"We're going out into the fields around the church tomorrow morning with baskets," said Amelia. Overhearing this topic of conversation, she and Evelyn had come closer. "The bower's to be made at the bottom of the garden. Evvy and I will sit in it during our wedding breakfast while everyone toasts us and offers their best wishes. You lads won't mind giving a hand, will you?"

"Of course not, Mellie, but why can't we get all the flowers we need from the garden?" Bicky asked.

"We can't have the borders chopped to pieces and trampled down, not when so many people will be seeing the gardens," said Egeria.

"That would be awful," Mellie agreed. "The garden must be perfectly lovely on our wedding day. I do hope the fine weather holds a while longer and it doesn't rain."

"You know how ladies are," Aubrey teased them. "A wedding's got to be perfect in every detail."

"I expect I'll feel dashed silly perched inside

the thing like the King and Queen of the May, but if it makes Mellie happy, then we'll do it," said Evelyn. He received a grateful kiss from his fiancée.

After the guests had refreshed themselves with cups of tea, Egeria invited them to rest in their rooms before dinner. "I'm afraid we're rather crowded with so many visitors. Daedelus, Icarus, we've put you two together. Kellynch, you and Freddie won't mind sharing, will you?"

"No, Aunt Egeria," said Kell, "that's quite all right. I've slept with Freddie before."

Dotty and Bicky grinned and Freddie tried to suppress a surprised laugh.

Egeria's expression didn't change as she answered, "Then you'll be comfortable."

As they left the drawing room, Phillip tried to slip out with the other young men, but his father said, "Wait a moment, Phil. We'd like to have a word with you."

Phillip cast an anxious look at Kell, but he had to obey the summons. Percival opened the door to his study across the wide central hall from the drawing room. Phillip went in. His parents followed. The door shut.

Freddie and Kell accompanied the party from Marsh Hall upstairs to be shown to their rooms.

"Poor old Phil," said Bicky. "I expect he's in for as awful a time as Uncle Winthrop gave you, Kell."

"It can't be as bad as that," Kell replied. "His father can't have him locked up 'til he behaves himself. Besides, Uncle Percy doesn't seem like the type to try it."

Once the butler Jermyn had shown Freddie and Kell to their room, they shut the door but could hear other members of the family in the hallway outside, calling happily to each other as they sorted out their baggage and settled into their own rooms nearby.

Kell flopped down on the bed near the window. "Aunt Eggie doesn't know it—and I certainly won't tell her—but I don't think I've actually shared a room with you since I was ten years old. You don't snore, do you?"

"You know I don't." Rather than have one of the maids put away his things, Freddie occupied himself with this task. He thought of his own manservant as he guessed which articles of clothing went where. Billy would know. He was careful to hang up his good shirt and morning coat in the wardrobe, as Billy had repeatedly reminded him to do before he'd left London that morning. The striped trousers went on a shelf by themselves; they would need to be pressed before he put them on.

"I'll feel dashed silly wearing this," he said as he placed the box containing his top hat on top of the wardrobe. "Topper and spats, like a brainless, inbred knut from before the war."

"The uniform of bloated capitalists and effete aristocrats," said Kell lazily. While he sympathized with most of his cousin's opinions, he wasn't as politically minded and had no desire to see the class he belonged to torn down. He said this last part aloud.

"I can't exactly call for the destruction of the upper classes either when it includes the people who are most dear to me," Freddie admitted.

"Mother's a brick," Kell agreed. "And I'm rather fond of Uncle Percy. He's a cut above the usual huntin', shootin', fishin' country squire. There's more in his head than second-hand opinions from conservative newspapers. Besides, he goes out of his way to make me feel welcome here. I can't say the same of Aunt Eg."

"It's not their personalities I object to. It's the style of living here and at Marsh Hall. Look at these enormous houses. A dozen Tollarhithes live in Foxgrove and over at the Vixen, with twice as many more servants to look after them. There are families in London who live crowded into one or two damp little rooms. If there isn't some sort of equitable balance between the rich and poor, then this country is headed for a bad crash, and we'll all suffer for it whether we deserve to or not."

"Well, it won't happen before this wedding–"

A loud knock startled them both; it hadn't come from the bedroom door, but the window. A decorative stone frieze about eighteen inches wide ran around the side of the building just beneath the first floor windows; Phillip was crouched on it. Kell leapt up and unlatched the window to let him in.

"I'm just two rooms down," Phillip reported as he climbed in over the sill. "Dotty and Bicky are in the one between us."

"Your talk didn't take very long," said Kell. "Did they give you a terrible scolding?"

"No, they didn't scold. That's not what they wanted." Phillip sat down in the window, fidgeted, and finally announced, "You might as well know: I'm going to be married."

"To *who*?" Kell demanded.

"You don't know her," Phillip explained. "I don't either. We've never met. She's Aunt Diana's niece, Josephine Montcliffe. She's only fifteen, so it'll be years before she's old enough. It's Mother's idea. She and Aunt Di are old friends and they've been planning this for a while. She says they'll have the girl down for a visit next summer, and won't I please come to meet her and be nice. But, you know, it didn't seem to me that Father was pushing very hard for it. He says they won't settle anything 'til after they see how we get on, and in any case we'd have to wait at least four or five years, which will give me plenty of time to grow up and get over this foolishness." He gave Kell an apologetic smile. "Father says that's more than fair."

"As fair as we can expect," Kell agreed. "It's certainly more understanding than my father's been. A lot can happen in five years. Maybe this girl will run off with somebody else."

Phillip's smile grew brighter. He held out a hand, and Kell went to him.

Freddie went out through the door, leaving the two alone.

On the terrace at the back of the house, he stopped to light a cigarette.

In its original form, the Jacobean Foxgrove had had two long wings flanking the sides of a courtyard. A century ago, these wings had been torn down and the courtyard made into a sunken garden. Below the terrace lay a large square of maze-like shrubbery with brick-lined paths converging on a fountain at the center. The borders were in bloom with late-summer flowers. Beyond spread a broad green lawn where workmen had set up long trestles and benches beneath a pavilion for the festivities that would follow the wedding ceremony. The workmen had also set up a bare wooden framework that Freddie guessed was meant for the bower. The bricks and stone of the demolished wings had been reused to form high walls around a series of smaller box-gardens on one side of this vast area, accessible through open archways, and the Vixen on the other, a scaled-down version of

Foxgrove in the same style, with its garden front at a right angle to the larger house.

Since he had more than an hour before he needed to dress for dinner, Freddie decided to take a walk. He tossed his cigarette butt into one of the enormous granite urns atop the terrace balustrade and went down the steps through the shrubbery and across the lawn. A stream ran through a carefully cultivated dell at the bottom of the garden, the rocks placed slightly better than nature could have managed to divert the water into decorative pools and tiny falls. Freddie took a footpath that ran beside it. The dell was full of bluebells in the spring and ferns in the summer, but even at this time of year it was a pretty walk.

When he came to a rustic-looking wooden bridge, he crossed it to enter the meadow on the other side and followed a path through the tall grass. As he passed a grove of trees, Freddie heard voices speaking before he was aware that anyone was nearby.

"Can you do it, Evvy? Can you end it this way?"

"Yes, I can! I have to."

A dark-haired youth emerged from the grove. Since he'd just heard Evelyn's voice, Freddie first thought that it must be he; then the boy turned and Freddie could see that it was a stranger. Evelyn emerged a moment later.

The boy stared at Evelyn with wide, softly brown eyes and said, "This isn't finished, Ev."

"It is finished," Evelyn answered. "I'm sorry, but it is."

The soft brown eyes looked hurt and angry, then the boy spat, "That's what you think! You'll be sorry, as sorry as I am to have met you. What a fool I was to trust a Tollarhithe!" He whirled and stormed off.

"Toby!" Evelyn called out, but the boy didn't turn back. Evelyn was about to go after him, until he noticed Freddie standing in the long shadows of the trees.

"I beg your pardon," said Freddie. "I didn't mean to eavesdrop. I didn't know anyone was here until it was too late. Who was that?"

"Just a friend," said Evelyn. "A village lad I know. His name's Toby Glovins."

"I don't think I've met him."

"Probably not. His father's the local butcher. You mustn't mind his manners. He sometimes loses his temper and says things he doesn't mean. We're the best of friends, really." Evelyn turned to watch as Toby climbed over a low stone wall at the edge of the meadow and headed toward Foxborough. "It doesn't matter. You won't see him again."

2

The next day was brilliantly sunny, with bright blue skies and only the slightest touch of autumnal coolness in the breeze. Freddie was reminded of the summer of 1914—not even ten years ago!—and the beautiful weather England had enjoyed just at the time the war had begun.

He went out that morning with the other young men and women to collect as many wildflowers as they could from the fields around Foxborough. These were available in plenty and a variety of bright colors: scarlet field poppies, blue harebells, yellow birdsfoot trefoil, and pale purple scabious.

The girls filled their baskets in the fields beyond the churchyard of St. Barnabas. Felix and Evelyn had joined them and their laughter could be heard even from a distance. Phillip and the younger Marsh boys had gone in quest of red campion in the shade of the oak woods. Freddie was left sitting alone, hacking at clusters of long-stemmed Michaelmas daisies with a pocket-knife.

When he'd gathered enough, he knotted a length of twine around each bundle before placing them into a basket. The sweet, sun-warmed scent of the flowers filled his senses. He shut his eyes.

At times, those months he'd spent in the trenches and in the hospital afterwards seemed like an incredible, horrible dream. And sometimes, *this* seemed like the dream. After all he'd been through in the war, days like this had a particularly dream-like quality. How could he be here again in the green Norfolk countryside, doing something as innocuous as gathering flowers? Yet even here, only a few yards away, was the church porch and the ornate memorial to the dead Tollarhithe sons and Foxborough men who would never come home.

When a shadow fell across him, he opened his eyes to find Kell standing over him, frowning with concern. "You're not tired, are you, Freddie?"

"No, I'm fine."

"Never mind the flowers. We'll go back to Foxgrove if you want to rest. I promised your Billy I'd look after you."

Freddie smiled; his cousin and manservant didn't like each other, but the two were united in their over-protective feelings for him. "You're doing a splendid job. Honestly, Kell, I haven't felt so well in a long time. You didn't hear a peep out of me all last night, did you? I slept like a rock. As a matter of fact, if you want to creep along the ledge and join Phil in his room tonight, I wouldn't mind."

"But that'd leave you alone, old thing," said Kell. "What if you had a bad turn and woke screaming in the night and nobody was there? Billy'd never forgive me." He grinned. "I could ask Phillip to come in with us. It might be a bit crowded, but I'm sure we could manage."

At midday, they carried their baskets of flowers into the garden to be placed in tubs of water to keep them fresh. Evelyn invited everyone to lunch at his father's house. Phaedra, who was mistress of the Vixen since her father-in-law was a widower, wasn't expecting so many people, but she had a quick word with the cook and a more than sufficient quantity of sandwiches and salad was set out on their terrace overlooking the lawn. The girls and Felix sat at one table, while Evelyn, Freddie and Kell joined Reginald, Phaedra, and Aubrey at another. The nursery maid had brought the baby outdoors and Phillip sat on a blanket spread on the paving stones to play with his nephew.

"You're very good with babies, Phil," his sister said after watching him babble and coo at little Peveril. "You could have one of your own someday."

"Me?" Phillip laughed. The baby, whom he was bouncing lightly on one knee, laughed too. "I can't see it."

"Give yourself time. You'll change your mind when you're a bit older. Sooner or later, every man wants a son to carry on his name."

"Not every man," said Kell.

"Most men," Phaedra responded. "It's only natural. Besides, after the terrible losses suffered during the war, it's our duty to have children. We must think of the future."

"'Our Daughters' England,'" Kell alluded to a

series of articles Phaedra had written under this title. During her pregnancy, she'd written in anticipation of having a daughter and described the greater freedoms and civic responsibilities she hoped this imagined child would see.

"Our sons' too," said Phaedra. "Their world will be very different from the one you and I grew up in, Kell Marsh. I'll do all in my power to see that Peveril never has to go through the horrors that we endured."

Kell couldn't argue with this. "You ought to stand for Parliament, Phee. You know how to give a speech."

"That's what I tell her," Reg said with pride.

Phaedra looked pleased, but said, "What party would I stand for? The Conservatives disapprove of my politics and would have me only because I'm a baronet's daughter. Labour is mostly hooligans and Bolsheviks, and the Liberals are twenty years behind the times. Perhaps in ten years, there'll be a feminist party and I'll consider it. Right now, I'm more interested in children." She turned to Evelyn. "You and Amelia will be having some."

"I certainly hope so."

"I expect that within a year of your wedding day– Oh! I forgot." Phaedra leapt up and went into the house.

"Phaedra's written some good articles lately," said Aubrey. "Have you read the one about how young women of the future will vote?"

"Why?" wondered Phillip. "Phee's got the vote now."

"But unmarried women under thirty don't," said Isolde from the other table. "She's pushing for us flappers. Pig's twenty-five, two years older than

Ev and Felix and certainly more sensible. I'm twenty-four. Why should they be able to vote while we can't?"

"I quite agree with you," said Felix. "It's most unfair."

"It's a pity we were too young to go and campaign for women's suffrage with her before the war," said Piggy. "It would've been marvelous fun to run riot in London, chucking bricks through MPs' windows and the rest of it."

"Don't be absurd," said Reg. "Phee never threw bricks or chained herself to anything. She's far too sensible and Uncle Percy wouldn't like it."

"I would've done it," replied Piggy, "if just for the thrill of being arrested."

"Actually, it was Mother who didn't approve of the suffragettes. She's always said that if a woman cares about politics, she should be clever enough to convince her husband to vote the way she wants." Phaedra returned with a small pile of letters which she placed on the table. "The post came while you were out," she explained to Evelyn. "There were more and some gifts, but Mellie's taken charge of those. These were addressed to you alone, so I set them aside. They must be from your particular friends."

Evelyn picked up the letters and began to open them one by one with his pocket-knife. "Yes, they're from my friends," he said after reading the first few. "Chaps who won't be here tomorrow but want to offer their congratulations."

"You'll have to answer them all," said his brother.

"I will, but I think that can wait 'til after the wedding," Evelyn laughed. "My friends will understand if I don't keep up with my correspondence." He stopped at one folded, sealed note; Freddie, who was seated at Evelyn's right, noticed that it was directed simply to 'Evelyn Tollarhithe' with no stamp or return address to indicate whom it was from. It must have been delivered by hand. Evelyn hastily tucked the square of paper into his coat pocket without opening it, then went on to read the rest of his letters.

Later that afternoon, the young people gathered to make garlands for the bower. While the other young men sat on the lawn, fishing flowers from tubs of water and trimming the stems, Felix carried their work to his girl-cousins, who sat at tables under the pavilion and wove them into long chains. He flirted with all of the girls simultaneously, but if he had special feelings for any one, he didn't reveal it.

"It's quiet," he observed when he returned to collect more flowers.

"What?" Evelyn asked, looking suddenly up. Although he worked quickly with his pocket-knife to trim the flower stems, he seemed distracted; he kept an eye on the sun as it sank lower over the brick wall to the west and would probably have spoken little if the constant chattering of the others didn't oblige him to answer.

"It's quiet," Felix repeated. "Where is everyone? You'd think they'd be out enjoying a fine evening like this."

"I'm certain that Mother and Auntie Di are sitting quietly somewhere discussing 'the problem'," said Phillip, referring to himself.

"Yes, I suppose they're all shut up indoors. My parents, Ev's father, Uncle Percy, the wedding guests— you lads excepted, of course," he added to Kell, Dotty, Bicky, and Freddie. "But you aren't dreary and old." Felix glanced up over the heads of the other boys toward the Vixen and smiled. "Phaedra and Reg."

"Phee and Reg aren't old and dreary," said Evelyn.

"They'll settle into it soon enough. It'll happen to you too, dear Ev. You'll sit home by the fire, smoking your pipe."

"I don't smoke a pipe. I sit home most evenings now, listening to the wireless in Father's study."

"But that's all you'll do," Felix went on teasing. "Every evening after dinner 'til bed-time. No more fun. No more going out to the pub or meeting your friends." Evelyn's face colored.

"Reg was always a dull sort of blighter," said Kell. "It's a mystery to me how he ended up with Phee. She's head and shoulders above him."

"That was her idea," said Evelyn. "She helped him after he lost his arm and decided that she ought to go on looking after him. Reg knows his luck, but I think he's intimidated by her."

"Aren't we all?" replied her little brother. "Phee's the cleverest of us. She ought've gone to the 'varsity. She would've made more of it than me or poor old Peter."

"Clement was the one she wanted to marry," said Piggy, who had come to see why Felix was taking so long.

"Did she?"

"Don't you remember, Phil, how she looked into this question of cousins marrying? That was because of Clement, not Reg. She read scientific journals, spoke to doctors when she served as a nurse in France. Phee told me that the fears are exaggerated." She cast a meaningful glance at Felix. "Unless you keep intermarrying like the Habsburgs, there's little danger your children will be born with two heads and nothing in either."

"Her baby seems perfectly sound," Phillip agreed.

"So she must've been right. When Clement was killed, that hit her rather hard, harder than she'd like to admit, especially so soon after Peter. Then Reg came home wounded. Besides, a girl's got to marry somebody. There simply aren't enough young men to go around anymore." Piggy picked up a wet bundle of flowers and returned to the pavilion. Felix didn't follow.

"Phaedra's baby hasn't made you change your mind about marriage?" Kell asked Phillip.

"I'm in no hurry to carry on the family name," Phil assured him. "Plenty of Tollarhithes as it is. I don't care if I'm a disappointment to them, Father as well as Mother. If they leave it up to me, this may be the last family wedding for quite some time."

"Where is Mellie, by the way?" Freddie wondered. "I haven't seen her in hours."

"She's finishing up the work on her wedding dress," said Felix.

"How long can it possibly take to sew on a piece of lace?" asked Kell in amazement.

"It's very delicate work. You have to see the dress to appreciate it. It's a sleeveless shift sort of thing in ivory with little straps at the shoulders and the low waist all the girls are wearing these days. The lace is in a long, triangular shape. What Mellie means to do is fasten the lace to the straps so that part of it goes down the front of the bodice in a foamy cascade..." Felix demonstrated by touching his own shoulders and fluttering one hand down his chest, "and the ends are flung back over her shoulders. If it hangs right, the effect should be lovely, like an angel's wings."

The other boys gaped at him.

"You spend too much time with the girls, old chap," said Dotty.

"I don't mind," Felix responded, unabashed. "*I* like girls." With that, he gathered up the bundle of flowers the boys had just completed and returned to the girls in the pavilion. He said something to them that the boys couldn't hear, but whoops of delighted laughter followed. Dotty's face turned bright red.

"Has he picked out one of 'em in particular?" Phillip wondered. "For all his talk against marriage, if Felix is going to be my brother-in-law one way or the other, I think I ought to know about it."

"I've no idea," said Evelyn. "He might marry one of my sisters just as easily as yours. I expect it'll be up to the girls in the end, and hope there won't be any hard feelings when they come to the point."

"He's right about one thing, Dotty," Bicky told his brother. "You won't get girls to like you if you don't spend time with them."

"How would *you* know?" Dotty retorted.

"At least, I've been out boating with a girl."

"And look how that turned out!"

"How did it turn out, Bicky?" Freddie asked. He knew that the two were referring to an adventure Bicky had had this past spring at Marsh Hall: he'd run off for an hour with Louisa Burke, evading the watchful eyes of her aunt long enough to tell the girl how he felt about her. Louisa had thanked him, but informed him that her affections were already bestowed elsewhere.

"I haven't seen Louisa since," Bicky said glumly. "I've written to her brother once or twice, asking after her, but I want to give her time to get Kell out of her mind."

"I'll be happy when she does!" Kell said with blunt sincerity. "She's a nice girl. She ought to marry the right sort of chap. I'm entirely the wrong sort. If I'd married her as Father wanted me to, I'd only make her miserable. If you can win her over, Bickers old chap, I'll give you both my blessing."

"Don't you ever think about marriage, Kell?" Evelyn asked him frankly. "I've heard, of course, about the trouble you had with your father. Wouldn't it be much easier to do what's expected, for your own sake? Have you never thought about children?"

"You mean, that son that a man naturally wants? Oh, I suppose I'll have to consider my duty to carry on the family name one of these days," Kell admitted with equal frankness. "But not for a long time yet." He flashed a smile at Phillip. "Not for at least ten years. If I do marry, it won't be to some poor, naïve girl who doesn't know why she won't be getting... well, what any wife has a right to expect. I can't pretend to feel something I don't. We'll have to agree: I won't trouble her about her private life as long as she doesn't interfere in mine."

"Do you believe you'll ever find such a girl?"

"Plenty of women would be happy to have such an arrangement if it means they'll be a viscountess."

"You wouldn't marry someone so mercenary."

"Perhaps not. All the same, I prefer to wait." Kell got up and walked away. Under the rose garden archway, he fished his cigarette case out of his coat pocket and lit one.

"I hope I didn't offend him," Evelyn said to Freddie. "I didn't mean to. I only... well, wondered."

"It isn't your fault," Freddie assured him. Evelyn had happened to strike a sensitive nerve. Neither Kell nor Phillip was at ease being among their families.

All summer, Freddie had watched Kell enjoying himself in London; he'd forgotten his problems and almost become the same careless, fun-loving boy he'd been before the war. The news of Phillip's planned engagement had put an end to that. Both were growing tense and unhappy. Kell seemed to feel it more deeply than Phillip did; it reminded him of what he already knew but didn't like to think about: they couldn't go on as they were forever. Put it off even by as much as ten years, but eventually they'd have to give in to family and societal pressures.

The last chain of flowers was finished as the sun sank out of sight behind the garden wall. Bicky and, at his brother's insistence, Dotty joined the girls and Felix to help hang the garlands up around the bower frame. Evelyn, who had been working swiftly to finish before sunset, put down the knife he'd been using to trim the flower-stems, washed the green stains from his hands in the water from one of the tubs, and hastily left. Phillip went over to Kell and the two began to talk quietly.

Freddie lay back on the grass and stared at the sky as twilight settled in. The color had waned from bright, cloudless blue to a dusky lavender, and was beginning to deepen. It was a beautiful evening, still, clear, and quiet. He could hear Kell and Phillip whispering together, and the smell of Kell's cigarette in the cooling air made him wish he had one of his own.

There was some animated discussion at the bower, then Felix, Piggy, and Perdita came to stand over him.

"The girls," announced Felix with a grin, "have a proposal."

"A dance!" cried Perdita. "There'll be lots of

dancing tomorrow. We need to practice."

"We need boys. We can't all dance with Felix," Alma said with her customary giggle, but she managed to claim Felix for her partner just the same.

"Come on, Freddie!" said Piggy, reaching down to take him by the hand and pull him up. "What could be more appropriate in the fox-grove than a spot of fox-trotting? Will that poor leg of yours be able to bear it?"

"If I don't jump about too much." He placed one hand on Piggy's waist and they tried a few tentative dance steps. The other couples who had paired off also began to practice, humming to provide their own music. "This is like a German picture Kell and I saw in London. There's a wedding party and a foxtrot breaks out among the guests."

"A German picture?" Piggy wrinkled her nose. "Aren't they all moody and strange with vampires and sleepwalkers?"

"Not all of them, dear Pig. This was a romantic comedy about an American heiress who marries a fortune-hunting prince. Kell enjoyed it and he hates gloomy films."

"We ought to have music," said Alma. "Could we hear Father's wireless if we put it out on the terrace and turned the sound up all the way?"

"They wouldn't like that at the house. It'd be far too loud," said her sister. "Besides, Father's in his study. He won't like to be interrupted. You know how he is when he's got something on his mind, and he's been positively brooding as Ev's wedding day gets closer."

"He doesn't object, does he?" Kell asked her. "He likes Mellie?"

"No, he's fond of Mellie. When Ev brought

her to the Vixen, he welcomed her just as if she were his daughter-in-law already. Only..." Isolde frowned, puzzled. "Something about it's worrying him."

"Kell, Phillip, come and join us!" Perdita called out to the pair at the archway. "Phil, where's your banjo? Did you bring it home with you?"

"I never took it to the 'varsity. It's somewhere in my room," her brother answered. "It's been so long since I've played it, I'm sure I've forgotten how. I'll sit your dance out, just the same."

"Oh, no, you won't," said Kell and pulled Phillip toward the lawn.

"Kellynch Marsh, that's not very gentlemanly of you!" Perdita protested. "We ought to be in proper pairs. If Evvy were still here..."

"Ev isn't here?" Amelia approached the group. "I thought he was with you."

"He left a few minutes ago," said Felix. "We thought he was going to find you. You've finished the work on your dress?"

"Yes, at last!" She looked up at the garland-covered bower. "What a wonderful job you've done. Thank you, all of you. If Evvy was going into the Vixen as I came out, we missed each other. He'll be out again in a minute or two. If you need a partner, Perdy, I'll stand in." She offered a hand, and the other girl took it. They began to dance.

Sir Percival emerged through a pair of French windows onto the Vixen terrace and stood watching the young people. When he realized that Phillip and Kell were paired, he looked surprised but said nothing. It was only when Phillip noticed that his father was there that he stepped quickly away from Kell.

"Father," Piggy cried out. "We want to have a dance. May we please bring out the gramophone?"

"Yes, of course, my dear, if you remember to take it back inside when you're done," Sir Percival answered his daughter, though his eyes were still on his son, who was headed toward the cover of the shrubbery. "Phillip," he called after him, when a sudden, shrill, horrified cry cut across the still evening. It came from the meadow beyond the garden.

The next few minutes were a riot of confusion. Everyone went in the direction of the scream. The meadow was full of people searching the tall grass in the fading light for a fallen or injured person, voices babbling, running together, as they all asked questions at once: "Who was it?" "What's happened?" "Has someone been hurt?" "Was it Evvy?"

Felix shouted, "Over here!" and ran toward a clump of trees, the same grove where Freddie had stumbled upon Evelyn and his friend Toby the day before.

Evelyn knelt beside Toby, who lay in the crushed grass. His hand was on Toby's chest; when he lifted it, the fingers were smeared with blood. The front of Toby's white shirt was dark with it. Evelyn looked up, dazed to find so many people around him.

Reginald, who was already at his brother's side, took his arm and tugged to urge him up. "Come away, Evvy!"

Evelyn was in hysterics. The girls screamed; the trees blocked their view of the dead boy, but they'd seen enough. Amelia stood staring in bewilderment after Evelyn as his brother dragged him away in the direction of their home. One of the younger boys was sick.

Sir Percival shouted over this chaos, trying to master the situation and restore order. "Felix! Get hold of yourself." He gave the stunned youth a shake to bring him to his senses. "Run to the Vixen, that's nearest, and telephone Mr. Thornton." Thornton was the Deputy Chief Constable for the county as well as a near neighbor. "The exchange will have the number. Tell him there's been an... accident. When he arrives, bring him here to me. The rest of you, return to Foxgrove. There's nothing you can do. Piggy dear, don't come any nearer. You shouldn't be here at all." But the young people remained where they were. "Go on! Phil, take your sisters and the other girls in. See that those boys go too. Help Dicky–Bicky– whichever one that is."

Amelia moved to help Dotty, who had fallen to his hands and knees. Phillip took one of the girls by the wrist and tried to shepherd the party toward the bridge.

Sir Percival turned to find Kell crouched beside the body. Freddie too had stepped closer. "What are you two up to?"

"We've been in battle, Uncle," Kell told him. "I've seen plenty of bodies before, much worse than this."

Freddie had seen dead bodies too, in the trenches or hanging on the barbed wire in No Man's Land. Boys younger than Toby. He felt a little queasy at the memory of that incredible, putrid stench, but he wanted to examine the scene. In spite of his previous experience of murders, he'd never before been on the spot like this. Toby Glovins looked surprisingly peaceful. Not horribly mangled nor bloody, except for the stain drying on his shirt.

Sir Percival bent down to have a look at the body himself. Night had fallen by this time and the grove was dark; he lit a match, which gave them a few seconds of light to see by until he had to put it out before he burned his fingers or dropped it in the grass. "Yes," he said. "He's certainly dead." He touched one cheek with the back of his hand. "Dead and cold, poor lad. I'll send a message to his family. They'll have to know of this tragedy. Oh, blast—and they'll hear about it from a Tollarhithe!"

Freddie didn't fully understand this last remark, but he was more surprised when Felix returned with Mr. Thornton and Percival told him, "It's Toby Glovins, the Foxborough butcher's son." He hadn't realized that Percival knew who the dead boy was.

Thornton, the local constable, and the doctor he'd brought with him, listened to what Sir Percival had to say about how the body had been found, and by whom.

"Young Evelyn," Thornton asked, "where is he now?"

"His brother's taken him home," Sir Percival answered. "He'll be there when you want to speak to him." While the doctor examined the body, Sir Percival drew Thornton aside for a private conference. "You lads can go."

Freddie, Kell, and Felix went obediently.

"It looks bad for Ev," Kell said as they walked back toward Foxgrove. "But I don't think..."

"No." Freddie believed that Evelyn's shock at finding his friend dead was genuine. If it were pretense, then Evelyn was much more cold-blooded than anyone would guess. Also, there were one or two odd things Freddie had noticed concerning Toby's death; he and Kell would have to discuss them when they had a chance.

"It's going to be awful for him, and Mellie too." They were in the garden now, passing the pavilion. "I wonder if there'll be a wedding tomorrow. Oh, I say, what's that?" Catching a glint of something metallic in the grass, Felix stooped to pick it up and held it up to see. "It's Evvy's pocket-knife."

Freddie and Kell exchanged a glance.

Inside Foxgrove, they met with further commotion. The group of young people had brought back the news of the dead youth, but could only report the little they'd seen before Sir Percival had sent them away. The ladies were all shocked and distressed, but they were also eager for more information and turned to the three young men who had just returned with a multitude of questions. Matilda, who was coddling her sickened son, wanted to know what had upset him so. Egeria demanded to know where her husband was. The girls were weeping, but Amelia was notably absent. So was Emily.

There was only a cold supper that night; the Foxgrove and Vixen cooks had been busy all day preparing for tomorrow's feast. Fresh fruit, bread, salads, cheese, ham, and chicken were set out on the dining room sideboard for the Tollarhithes and their guests to take as they chose. In light of this unexpected tragedy, most were too disturbed to think of food. Freddie picked up an apple and decided to go to his room. It was early, but he wanted to be away from the noise and crowd to think.

He went up the stairway to the guest bedrooms; a window on the landing looked out over the gardens. Here, Freddie paused, for he'd caught a glimmer of lights in the darkness outside. A procession of men was crossing the distant meadow, some bearing torches or lanterns, others carrying a makeshift stretcher. They were bringing Toby's body in.

The door nearest the landing opened and Emily peeped out. "Is that–? Oh, Freddie, I was hoping it might be you. Step into my room for a moment, please."

"Yes, of course, Aunt Emily."

When he entered his aunt's room, he found Amelia there, curled in a chair. She clutched a handkerchief in one hand and looked as if she'd been crying.

"There was such a lot of screaming and to-do, I thought it best to take poor Mellie away," Emily explained. "She's told me what happened, how Evelyn was found with the dead boy. Freddie, this is awful! I never thought we'd have to endure anything like this again. You don't think Evelyn's done this dreadful thing, do you?"

"No, I don't believe he did."

Amelia lifted her eyes to him. "Do you really?" she asked. "You aren't just saying so to be kind and comfort the ladies? Tell us honestly, Freddie, please."

"I don't," Freddie answered sincerely. "I have reasons to doubt it."

"Good!" Emily gave her niece a triumphant look. "I told you, Mellie, didn't I? Freddie, I want you to investigate this murder. If Evelyn isn't responsible, there must be some proof of it, or proof that someone else killed that boy. I want you to find it."

"Me, Aunt Emily?"

"Who better?" his aunt responded. "It was wonderful how you exonerated Kell. And he's told me that you boys had a hand in solving that awful business with your cousin Wilfrid and that poor girl who'd been strangled. Will you look into this, for Evelyn's sake?"

Freddie turned to Amelia. "Do you want me to,

Mellie? After how badly it turned out the last time I intervened?"

"I never blamed you, Freddie," said Amelia. "What happened to my sister wasn't your fault. I think that it would've ended just the same sooner or later even if you hadn't been there, except that you helped Kell and me. If you can help Evvy now, I'll be grateful."

3

The night was a long and restless one. Freddie and Kell stayed up late talking and went down to breakfast the next morning later than the usual hour. Sir Percival was just coming out of the dining room as the two arrived; his expression brightened at the sight of Freddie.

"Ah, there you are," he said. "I want a word with you." Freddie let himself be led into the library. Since Percival wasn't interested in speaking with him, Kell went to get his breakfast.

Sir Percival shut the door. "I've been talking with Emily," he began. "She tells me she's engaged you to look into this... ah, unfortunate incident."

"Not 'engaged,' precisely," Freddie answered. "She and Mellie have asked for my help. They want to see that Evelyn isn't falsely accused of his friend's death. I've agreed to do it for Mellie's sake and Evelyn's, and for the sake of the family."

"I'm pleased to hear that you look at it that way," Sir Percival said with keen appreciation. "It is indeed the family we have to think of, and not only Evelyn. After the scandal at Marsh Hall with Kell falling under suspicion, I won't have the same repeated here. I don't wish to speak ill of my sister's husband, but anyone can see that Winthrop handled that whole business very badly and made matters worse. I want no arrests made 'til we're certain we have the right culprit, and I mean to be quite sure. I've had a word with Thornton and he's agreed to leave Evelyn free. We'll keep an eye on him 'til the matter is cleared up. The boy's very upset. You saw how he was. The doctor had to sedate him. Aubrey tells me that Reginald sat up all night at his bedside. Well, to come to the point: Emily says you've done this before. You were the one who saw Kell out of trouble, isn't that so? She seems to think you can do some good here too." He leaned closer to the young man and asked in a lowered tone, almost as if it were an extremely personal inquiry, "Can you, Freddie? Do you see a way to learn who's responsible for what happened to Toby Glovins?"

This seemed a strangely roundabout way of asking the question. "Isn't that for the police to investigate?"

"Oh, they'll do their job. Our local constabulary's never had a murder before, but Thornton sent for an inspector from Weymondham. I'm sure they'll do their utmost."

Freddie was confused by Sir Percival's reticence. What exactly did his uncle want him to do? Did he have suspicions of his own about who had killed Toby and wanted them examined, not by the police, for whom justice was the first priority, but by someone connected with the family? Did he believe that one of the Tollarhithes was responsible? "You don't think it's Evelyn, do you?"

"No, I don't," Sir Percival answered so promptly that Freddie was sure he was speaking the truth. "There are already certain points in Evelyn's favor. You may have noticed them yourself."

"Yes, I have." He and Kell had discussed the scene of the murder at length the night before. "For one thing, Toby hadn't just died."

"Exactly! The blood wasn't fresh. Now, I've never seen a murdered man before, but I've shot plenty of game and I know how quickly blood dries. Toby's shirt was stiff with it. Kell, with his great experience of bodies on battlefields, would surely tell you just the same."

Freddie had to smile. Kell had said precisely that.

"I touched the poor lad's cheek myself, you remember. He was already cool. They tell me that his body was quite cold and stiffening when they carried it in," Percival went on. "I'll wager the coroner finds that Toby died at least a half an hour before we saw him. Evelyn was in the company of a number of people, yourself included, at that time. You went out to the garden together, didn't you?"

"Yes, right after we had our tea," Freddie confirmed. "Evelyn was with us all the time until he got up and left..." To meet Toby, just as he'd done the night before? From what Freddie had overheard, it had sounded as if that last meeting was indeed their final one. But why else would Evelyn have gone there again? "That was just before you and Mellie came out to us."

"How long after Evelyn left did we hear him scream?"

"I don't think it could've been more than ten minutes later."

"There, you see! It isn't possible for Evelyn to have done this. Then there's the knife."

Freddie nodded. "Evvy had none with him. He left his in the grass near the pavilion. Felix found it afterwards. There was no knife in the wound."

"The police are searching for it now. Mind you, I don't think they'll find it. It seems to me that someone must've taken it away."

"Do you have any idea who?" Freddie asked.

"That'll be something for you to find out." Percival gave Freddie a brisk pat on the shoulder and opened the library door. "Go and have your breakfast, then we'll begin this investigation of yours."

Freddie hadn't expected to find very many people in the dining room, but when he went in, a number of the family were there: Emily had gone, but Matilda and Egeria were still at breakfast, as were Piggy and Perdita. Great-Uncle Archibald sat alone at the far end of the table, and Kell was at the opposite end, nearest the sideboard.

After missing their dinner, the ladies were ravenous and eager to talk about the murder in the meadow. The initial shock had faded; none of them had known Toby Glovins and their distress at his death was more a feeling of general horror and astonishment than personal grief. As they so often repeated to each other, to think that such a thing could happen at Foxgrove! All were quite certain that Evelyn could have nothing to do with it.

"Honestly," said Egeria as she encouraged Freddie to help himself to bacon and eggs from the sideboard. "I don't know what England's coming to. It's as if all the awful things going on in other parts of the world since the war have come in and made everyone behave in the most strange ways. Girls demanding that boys marry them." At first, Freddie thought that the lady was referring to his cousin Angela's recent, hasty marriage, until Egeria added in a lower, confidential tone, "Amelia wrote to Evelyn, you know, and told him to come for her rather than wait for him to propose. Most forward, I call it. And boys..." She glanced at Kell and her face colored. Freddie understood what she was alluding to. So did Kell. "Not even in secret, but out in the open for everyone to talk about. And now there are these terrible murders in our midst! It's the end of all decency as we know it."

Freddie was trying to think of a tactful reply, when Kell said, "I can't approve of murder, Aunt Eggie, but I don't see anything indecent about the rest of it."

"You wouldn't, Kellynch Marsh," Egeria retorted. "When the proper way of doing things is destroyed, who knows what will happen next?" Having delivered this dire warning, she left the room.

Archibald, who had been quiet, suddenly looked hard at Kell and announced, "I can tell you one thing, these fancy-lad doings of yours wouldn't have been allowed in my day."

"Oh, I'm sure it went on even then," Kell rejoined.

"It may have done, but we would've put a stop to it," Archibald told him with severity. "In my day, a young man knew his responsibilities. He knew what was right, and if he didn't, his family saw to it he learned it soon enough."

Another young man might have been intimidated, but after his difficulties with his own father, Kell felt equal to face any disapproval. "Then I'm very glad we aren't living in your day anymore."

The elderly man glared at him, deliberately put down his fork on his unfinished plate of eggs, and left the room in disgust. The ladies looked extremely uncomfortable.

"Thank goodness that horrid old man's leaving today," said Matilda. "Going back to his cottage, Egeria tells me. It'd be unbearable to sit at the same table with him for every meal."

"Where is Phil, by the way?" asked Kell. He had knocked on Phillip's door on the way down to breakfast, but there'd been no answer.

"He's gone out with my boys to watch the police search the meadow," said Matilda, relieved to change the subject. "I can't imagine why. You'd think they'd never want to be near that awful place again!"

"Search the meadow?"

"For the knife," Freddie said. "It hasn't been found yet."

"Aunt Emily's gone out too," said Piggy.

"Not to watch the police. She's sitting in the garden," Matilda added. "Theresa might be with her. She spent last night with Mellie over at Aubrey's house, you know. The poor girl's so terribly distressed by all of this and who can blame her? We've been busy already this morning, sending messages to the wedding guests who wouldn't have heard the news yet, cancelling reservations. Emily's wired your father, Kell, to say he needn't come."

"Have you heard?" Perdita asked Freddie and Kell. "There's to be no wedding today."

"Postponed," Piggy told them. "Mellie and Ev can't think of marrying while he's under this awful suspicion. They'll have to wait. Poor Mellie."

"Poor Evvy!" said her sister.

Kell and Freddie hadn't heard this news officially, but both assumed that the wedding would be cancelled or delayed under the circumstances.

The others finished their breakfasts and went out into the garden. Kell remained to wait for Freddie.

"When you're done, why don't we see what the police are up to?" he suggested. "Find out what they know. It's as good a place as any to start if you're going to do as Mother asked."

"I'm going to do more than that," Freddie replied. "I've been given a special task: Uncle Percy wants me to investigate Toby's murder as well... only, I'm not sure it's for the same reasons that Aunt Emily and Mellie do."

Kell grinned. "And we're going to help you, aren't we, Phil and I?"

"Yes, of course. I couldn't manage without you."

They went out through one of the garden doors. Before they descended from Foxgrove's terrace, Freddie observed two large, official-looking vehicles parked in the meadow; a number of uniformed policemen and men in plain clothes were busy in the grove and searching the tall grass. He looked around to find Reginald on the end of the Vixen terrace nearest the meadow, also watching the police and smoking his pipe. Felix was perched on top of the rose-garden wall beside Dotty and Bicky, his towhead bright in the morning sunlight. The ladies all appeared to be gathered in the shade of the pavilion, where they couldn't see the meadow but were near the focus of activity and could immediately receive any fresh news. Sir Percival was nowhere to be seen.

Kell accompanied Freddie as far as the lawn, then went in search of Phillip. Emily, who'd been watching for Freddie, came toward him. "Pal's speaking to the policeman in charge of this terrible business. He wanted you to join them," she said. "I've heard he's asked you to look into things, too."

It took Freddie a moment to understand that

she was speaking of Sir Percival; 'Pal' was a pet name that only his sister and Aubrey ever used. "Yes, he agrees that Evelyn couldn't have killed his friend Toby, and wants to be certain that the guilty party is found."

"Mellie will be relieved to hear it. Pal's patronage will be of enormous help in clearing matters up. His authority will make it so much easier for you to ask questions of people, but..." she hesitated, then took Freddie's arm and spoke softly, "I'm afraid that my brother has always been a little too concerned with the appearance of things. He mightn't be as interested in the truth behind this boy's death as much as how it looks."

"I think that he thinks it's one of the family," Freddie murmured in response. "Not Evelyn, but someone else. I can't yet tell who."

His aunt looked alarmed. "I hope you're wrong, Freddie. It would be too terrible if you were right. Ah, Mellie, my dear," she turned to Amelia, who had emerged from the pavilion. "You be glad to hear that Evelyn isn't in as great a danger as we feared."

The girl looked relieved and said to Freddie, "But surely you couldn't have done so much already."

"I've barely done a thing," Freddie admitted. "As it happens, Uncle Percival is certain that Ev is innocent." He didn't tell her his suspicions; it must be enough for Amelia to know that Evelyn was safe. "I'm sorry about your wedding, Mellie."

If this day had gone as planned, the wedding party would have assembled at the church by this hour and the ceremony would be underway. A wedding breakfast would have followed, and the celebration would've gone on through the afternoon and into the evening, long after the newlywed couple had departed for their honeymoon. The pavilion would be crowded with party guests, a hired band would be playing dance music, and the bower they'd decorated yesterday wouldn't be sitting empty.

"Thank you, Freddie." Amelia gave him a small, grateful smile. "I'd marry Evvy today regardless, to show I haven't abandoned him in his troubles, but everyone says it's best to wait. We shouldn't begin our lives together under a shadow."

"You won't have to wait too long, my dear," said Emily encouragingly. "This matter will soon be cleared up, at least as far as Evelyn is concerned. We won't keep you any longer, Freddie."

Freddie made his way onto the path beside the stream. Once he went down into the dell, his view was blocked by trees but he could hear Sir Percival's voice. The baronet was speaking about him to someone, presumably Mr. Thornton:

"–a nephew of mine from London. Fancies himself a detective and he's actually gained something of a reputation for it. He's had some small experience with murder investigations. It's right you know that I've engaged him to look into matters in the family's interest. He won't interfere with police business, but I trust you'll give him whatever assistance you can. Ah, here he is."

Thornton wasn't the only police official in conference with the baronet on the meadow side of the bridge; Inspector Deffords was also present.

Deffords smiled wryly as the younger man appeared. "Yes, I know Mr. Babington."

"John, hello!" Freddie greeted him. "When I heard that someone was coming from Wymondham, I hoped it'd be you."

Sir Percival was surprised by this use of a first name. "Ah, you're acquainted?"

"Inspector Deffords investigated Bertie's death, and we've worked together since then," Freddie explained. Now that he had identified the inspector as his friend, his uncle would be less inclined to see Deffords as an outsider.

The Deputy Chief Constable, however, regarded Freddie with curiosity. If he resented this intrusion into his professional domain, he didn't show it; Freddie thought Thornton was probably used to deferring to Sir Percival, as anyone who lived around Foxborough must be. At least, his previous work with Deffords would establish that he wasn't simply a meddling amateur. "What sort of assistance can we give you, Mr. Babington?"

"I suppose you can begin by telling me what you've learned so far," Freddie answered. "I wouldn't like to go over the same ground twice."

Thornton chuckled. "Oh, we've been over the same ground more than once this morning." He seemed to think this a good joke. "But I take it you mean the facts in the case? Very well then. Tobias Glovins, aged 23, elder son of the butcher in Foxborough, was killed last night shortly before sunset in that grove of trees over there. I suppose he was waiting for someone..." Thornton cast a glance at Sir Percival.

"You'll have a chance to question Evelyn," said Percival. "His father agrees he's fit to speak to you this morning."

Thornton nodded, then continued to Freddie, "It looks as if there'd been a struggle in the trees. The murdered lad had grass stains on his trousers and his shirt sleeve was torn. Dr. Preston, who examined the body, tells me that he was stabbed to the heart by a short, sharp knife. That's all we can say about it 'til we see it for ourselves."

"Then the knife hasn't been found yet?"

"Not yet, no."

"I brought some men with me," Deffords added, nodded to indicate the police working in the meadow. "They'll go over every inch of ground, but I don't expect they'll find much. No hope of footprints with so many people trampling over the place. No fingerprints unless we find that missing knife. My sergeant's gone to Foxborough to question the butcher's family and have a look through the victim's room."

"I called on the Glovinses myself this morning," said Thornton. "They had, ah, one or two things to say about who's to blame for the lad's death, but nothing we can consider a serious accusation." He was deliberately vague, but both Percival and Freddie understood: the Glovinses blamed the Tollarhithes.

Percival nodded. "I understand that Mr. Glovins must naturally be extremely upset at losing his son."

"Yes, sir," Thornton agreed. "It was heartbreaking to see such a great, hearty man struck so low by grief. The younger boy and girl are little better. This isn't the only worry they have to bear. There's another boy missing, Benny Wegman, the butcher's apprentice. He never came home last night from his work and no one knows what's become of him. I've sent a pair of constables out to search the neighborhood and alerted police around the county."

That the butcher's son should be killed on the same night as his apprentice disappeared must be more than a coincidence; Freddie wondered just how the two were connected.

"We'd like to talk to young Evelyn now if you've no objection, Sir Percival," Thornton requested.

Sir Percival had none, and accompanied the two men to the Vixen.

Freddie didn't go with them. He wanted to talk to Evelyn himself, but not with police present. He also wanted to consult Felix; Felix was the one person Freddie thought he could freely discuss a certain delicate aspect of this case with.

As he approached the foot of the rose-garden wall, the boys atop looked down. "Good morning, Freddie," Dotty said cheerfully. "We were just watching you and Uncle Percy chatting with the Deputy Constable and that inspector chappie. Isn't he the same one who came to Marsh Hall when Bertie went into the river?" Freddie confirmed that it was. "And you're investigating this too, Freddie?"

"Yes, both Aunt Emily and Uncle Percival have asked me to."

"You aren't going to go around accusing all your nearest relations of murder again, are you?"

"I hope not!" Freddie tried to match his cousin's joking tones, but he was sincere.

"It ought to be easier for you this time," said Bicky. "No one can refuse to answer your questions without looking odd in Uncle Percy's eyes."

"What did you want to ask us, Freddie?" added Dotty. "You know just where we were when all this happened."

"Actually, it was Felix I wanted to speak to."

The two brothers exchanged exaggerated looks of alarm. "Watch out, Felix," Dotty warned him.

"You're Evelyn's closest friend," Freddie explained to Felix. "I thought you'd be the one to ask about him and this Toby."

Felix regarded him for a moment, then said, "Yes, all right. Ask away. Don't worry," he told the two Marsh boys. "Freddie won't have me arrested. He knows precisely where I was when Toby died too." He climbed down from the wall and he and Freddie walked a little distance away so they could speak privately.

"Did you know Toby Glovins?" asked Freddie.

"I was with Ev when he first met Toby, as a matter of fact. That was about three years ago, the summer after the war. We went to the pub in Foxborough, and Toby was there with his brother. They'd just come to town."

"Are they a new family? I'd heard that Toby's father was the Foxborough butcher."

"He is," answered Felix. "They only came to live here recently. The father was a local lad who went to Canada ages ago, married a girl of French extraction. She'd passed on before he came back to his old home, but the younger son is named Thibault and there's a daughter, Victoire. Tibby and Torie, they call 'em. When we first met, Toby and his brother said they'd heard some awful tales about how high-and-mighty the Tollarhithes were and we did our best to show them it wasn't true. We went out of our way to make them feel welcome—bought rounds of beer, played darts, that sort of thing. We talked about the war. Toby'd been in some Canadian regiment and at least set foot in France before the end of it, which is more than Ev or I can say we did."

"Evvy and Toby became friends right away?"

"Oh, yes, great friends." Felix paused, then added in a lower voice, "More than friends, if that's what you wanted to ask me about."

Freddie nodded. "I wondered if it weren't so. I discovered them by accident in that same grove when I was out for a walk the night before last."

"They used to meet there. I didn't realize they still were."

"Did you know about it from the beginning?"

"Ev's never kept secrets from me." Felix shrugged. "You know how it is. We're packed off to school before we're of an age to notice girls and spend the next eight or ten years seeing nobody but other boys, making special friendships, and fending off the older lads. Then it's off to 'varsity where you still don't have much chance to meet girls. I think girls are nicer myself, but there's only so much a decent chap can do. A kiss or two, really. Unless you're an awful cad or bounder, you simply can't play around with them the way you do with other boys. Everybody does it, but some boys take it more seriously than others."

"Toby took it more seriously than Evelyn?"

"Ev was the one getting married and Toby didn't like it." Felix shook his head. "I can see why someone might want Toby out of the way to avoid a scandal, but killing him seems an awfully cruel way of doing it. Whoever did must've wanted to be sure he was gone for good."

This confirmed Freddie's impression that Toby's killer might very well be one of the Tollarhithes. "I'd like to talk to Evelyn. Do you think he's up to it?" If Percival had allowed the police to see Evelyn, then surely he wouldn't be barred.

"They won't say no to Uncle Percy's own official investigator." Felix smiled. "I'll go with you."

They were crossing the lawn toward the Vixen when a flutter of excitement went through the group of ladies in the pavilion; Sir Percival, Thornton, and

Deffords had just emerged from the house. Amelia seized her mother's hand and looked alarmed. The Tollarhithe girls and Marsh ladies didn't dare to ask about the outcome of Evelyn's interview, but Egeria went to speak to her husband. After a few quiet words from Percival, the lady smiled.

"It's quite all right," she announced.

After Thornton and Deffords had gone, Evelyn himself came outside with his father. The young man looked pale and shaken and gazed around the garden uncertainly, as if he were afraid the people there would shun him.

Amelia met him at the foot of the terrace steps and would've thrown her arms around him, but Evelyn drew back from her attempted embrace.

"Evvy, darling..." She reached out hesitantly to try and take his hand instead. "Don't be afraid. It's all right."

"Is it?"

"Yes, of course. None of us believes it." She glanced over her shoulder at Freddie. "We're doing all we can to prove it isn't true. We will prove it, and then no one can say a thing against you."

Evelyn let out a strange, hard laugh. "Oh, you mean Toby's murder!"

"Yes." Amelia looked puzzled. "What else?"

"You haven't heard it all yet," said Evelyn. "It's not so bad as saying I killed Toby, but it's awful in its way. It'll be just as bad for you. You'll hate me for what I've done."

"I couldn't hate you, Ev, no matter what."

"But you don't know! If you haven't heard the gossip about why I went to that grove last night, what Toby was doing there, you will soon enough. Didn't you wonder about it?"

"Well, yes, I did," she admitted.

"You needn't wonder any longer!" cried Evelyn. "They'll say I killed him to keep him quiet, but there's no keeping it quiet anymore." His voice rose shrilly, hysterically. If anyone hadn't been listening to him before, they couldn't help it now. "Do you understand? Can you? You've had a lucky escape. Oh, Mellie, please go away. I can't bear you to look at me."

Amelia continued to stare at him in disbelief. Since she didn't go away, Evelyn did. He put up one arm to cover his face and fled back into the house. Amelia stood where she was for a long, stunned minute. The garden was absolutely quiet. As the girl turned to look around at all the people who had witnessed this scene, tears shone in her eyes.

Theresa went to her daughter's side. "Hush, dearest. Come with me." She led Amelia away toward Foxgrove.

"Oh, that ridiculous boy!" Emily said in exasperation. As she followed the mother and daughter, Freddie and Felix went into the Vixen.

4

Evelyn was in his bedroom, sitting on the foot of the bed with his head down on his drawn-up knees. He looked up, startled, when Felix tapped lightly on the ajar door and said, "May we come in, please? Freddie wants to talk to you."

"What about?" Evelyn asked hoarsely.

"He's investigating Toby's murder," Felix explained as he ventured into the room. "Uncle Percy's engaged him specially."

Evelyn made a laughing, sobbing sound. "Have you come to accuse me, Freddie?"

"No," Freddie assured him. "I only want to know about your friend, Toby Glovins. Felix has explained things to me."

"Yes, everyone knows now, even the police. Even Mellie." He sobbed again. "It was all in fun! I was fond of Toby, but I always meant to marry Mellie. We've said so since we were children. I never concealed that from Toby. He knew it couldn't go on. I broke off with him the day I received Mellie's letter, told him we had to end it before I went to Marsh Hall to settle things with her. I've had nothing to do with him since."

"But you have been meeting with him," said Freddie.

"To talk!" Evelyn insisted. "I wanted to explain. I hoped we might still be friends, but Toby wouldn't understand." He looked up at the two young men standing before him. "Do you think he expected me to continue seeing him after I'd married, like one of Kell's private arrangements? Or that I'd go on with him and never marry? A Tollarhithe and the butcher's son. Imagine the scandal." His eyes grew wide as he considered the more horrific scandal he was actually in the midst of. His head fell into his hands. Felix sat down beside him and patted his back.

When Evelyn lifted his head to wipe the tears from his face with the back of one hand, Freddie gave him a handkerchief and asked, "Did you arrange to meet Toby last night? You went out to the grove, knowing he would be there."

"Yes, I had a note from him. I still have it." Evelyn felt vaguely at his pockets. "I showed it to Mr. Thornton..." He looked at a folded piece of paper lying on the small table at his bedside.

Freddie picked it up, recognizing it as the same

note he'd seen Evelyn receive at lunch yesterday. He unfolded it to read the message: *By sunset. Please, one last time.*

He read the words aloud, and Evelyn explained, "That was our usual place, you see. But I was a little late because we were cutting all those flowers and couldn't get away until the sun was actually down. When I got there, I found him. Toby...dead! I thought he'd done it himself, because of me, 'til Reg told me that they couldn't find the knife." He blotted his eyes and blew his nose. "I saw the looks on their faces—Thornton's and that other policeman."

"You didn't actually *tell* them about you and Toby?" Felix asked incredulously.

"The police? No. I'm not quite that stupid, but I'm sure they guessed what it was all about. Uncle Percy's done his best to protect me, but he must despise me now. I suppose you despise me too."

"No," said Freddie, although he couldn't help thinking that Evelyn hadn't behaved very well toward either Toby or Amelia.

"I do love Mellie, you know," Evelyn told him. "I'm not a confirmed pansy like Kell. I couldn't live that way. I want to be married to a nice girl and have children and all the rest of it. I meant to be a proper husband to her, though she'll never believe that now. It wasn't bad enough that I deceived her—I've humiliated her. She'll never forgive me."

"Ev, honestly, I don't think Mellie would mind so much if it had ended when you said it did," Felix said comfortingly.

"Did it?" Freddie asked.

Evelyn began to weep again.

"Enough of that, Freddie Babington!" Reginald was at the door, glaring at him furiously. "Father told me you'd come up here after Evvy, but I'd no idea you were questioning him this way. What do you think you're doing?"

"Uncle Percival has engaged me to investigate this murder," Freddie answered.

"Well, my brother didn't do it!" He seized Freddie with his single hand to pull him out into the hallway. "Investigate all you like," Reginald hissed, "but leave Evvy out of it. Hasn't he suffered enough? The Tollarhithes have never seen such a scandal, and all over Toby Glovins. If that miserable little wretch had known his proper place and kept to it, we wouldn't be in this mess."

"If he got ideas above himself," Freddie spoke with a hint of sarcasm, "didn't Evelyn encourage him?"

"What if he did? These things will happen. Toby should've had the decency to go away once he saw that Evvy was done with him. I don't say he deserved to die, but he only has himself to blame for it. He was a troublemaker, hanging about when he wasn't wanted, making threats."

"Threats?" echoed Freddie.

"Didn't you know? He meant to spoil things for Ev and make a scandal of their friendship. Evvy told me so last night. Toby promised to put a stop to the marriage if he could."

"He seems to have done that," Freddie murmured. "Very well. I only have one last question, Reg, and then I'll leave."

"I told you, enough."

"Not for Evelyn…for you."

"Me?"

"The rest of us were in the garden when we heard Evelyn scream," said Freddie. "We all ran at once toward the meadow and found him. But you were already at Evelyn's side, ahead of everyone else. How did you reach him so quickly?"

The flushed, angry red color drained from Reginald's face. He turned suddenly and paced away down the hall.

"If you don't wish to tell me," Freddie called after the retreating man, "I'm sure Mr. Thornton will be interested."

Reginald stopped. "You wouldn't."

"I told you: I'm acting as Uncle Percy's special investigator," Freddie said as he went after Reginald. "He wants this done discreetly and I mean to be discreet. If there's no reason for the police to know about it, then I won't tell them, but I must have the truth from you." He hadn't intended to use the authority he'd been given this way, but he wasn't going to let Reg walk away without giving him an explanation. This point had been puzzling him since last night.

Reginald gaped at Freddie as if he'd never seen him before. When he pulled himself together, he said, "There's no reason you shouldn't know. Tell Uncle Percy. Tell the police if you like. I was there with Evelyn ahead of everyone else because I followed him. While you were all making merry in the garden, I was on the terrace, keeping my eye on Evvy. When I saw him leave, I went after him."

"You knew where he was going?" asked Freddie.

"I knew he meant to meet Toby. I saw him receive a note at lunch yesterday. You did too, didn't you? I noticed you looking at it, sticking your nose into other people's business even before you had an excuse. You didn't know what that note meant, but I did. I've seen others like it. I knew exactly where Evvy was going and I meant to put a stop to it."

"Stop it?"

"Oh, nothing like that!" Reginald insisted. "I didn't kill Toby, if that's what you're thinking. I wanted to convince Ev to come back with me, not to see Toby. What was he thinking, the night before his wedding? But Ev was already at the grove before I caught up with him. I saw him go in among the trees and a moment later, I heard him scream." He laughed sourly. "At first, I thought that Toby had hurt him. I ran to help my brother, and I found him kneeling beside that boy's body."

"Freddie."

When Freddie left the Vixen, he headed toward Foxgrove along a path that skirted the outer garden wall. Inspector Deffords stood waiting for him. "I thought you'd gone."

"I had some business with my men before they packed up, but I wanted to talk to you before I went into Foxborough." He offered a cigarette and Freddie was grateful to take it; he hadn't had one since before breakfast.

"I can't say I'm surprised to find you in the middle of this," Deffords told him. "Not after that business with Bertram Marsh, then the Putey girl who was mixed up with your cousin Wilfrid. Now a body turns up in your uncle's back garden."

"Do you mind that Uncle Percy's engaged me?" asked Freddie.

"I won't object. I can't if Sir Percival insists and my superiors allow it, and they do. Even the higher-ups know to stay on the good side of the local nobs, and not just where murder's concerned. As long as everybody important in Norfolk is an uncle of yours, I might as well make use of it. I know how your class closes ranks. Sir Percival's family won't tell me a thing, but they'll tell you. You can ask them questions. Play detective all you like, but I want you to be careful. It's safer to stay out of murders. I've said so before."

"It couldn't be avoided this time. I was in it before it'd happened. We were all together in the garden when we heard Evelyn scream." He told Deffords the circumstances of how the body had been discovered, then clarified who precisely he meant by "we." He explained the relationships between the numerous Tollarhithes and those members of the Marsh family the inspector was already familiar with. Deffords made careful notes. "I'm not investigating the murder, as such. Aunt Emily's asked me to clear Evelyn of suspicion, and Uncle Percy is interested in ensuring that the Tollarhithes aren't involved in Toby's death. If your investigation turns up evidence that he was stabbed because of a drunken quarrel or something of the sort with a local ruffian, then my work is done."

"There's one Tollarhithe you don't need to worry about." Deffords lit a cigarette for himself before he confided, "When I first arrived, Mr. Thornton told me privately that if we find any evidence of what he calls 'a special friendship' between Evelyn Tollarhithe and the dead lad, we're to disregard it."

Freddie was astonished. "You mean you're not allowed to suspect Evelyn?"

"I'm here to find a murderer, not dig up a morals charge against a baronet's nephew. Lord Marshbourne might've done the same for his son last spring if the two of them hadn't quarreled about it just before Bertram Marsh was killed. I'd rather not have the same muddle over secrets again. I wasted a lot of time on Captain Marsh because no one would tell me the truth."

Freddie realized that Deffords was saying this to let him know that he understood exactly what had happened at Marsh Hall and why Freddie had defended his cousin so desperately. "As long as such unfair laws exist," he said, "you can't expect people to speak freely to policemen."

"You won't have to lie this time to protect anybody," Deffords told him bluntly. "If we find any real evidence against Evelyn Tollarhithe, I won't hesitate to arrest him for murder. As it stands, he's out of the running. The doctor who examined the body says that Toby Glovins died around half-past six. Sunset yesterday was at six minutes past seven."

"Then he was killed at least half an hour before Evelyn left us."

"That's right. Evelyn Tollarhithe has ten witnesses to say where he was at the time of the murder. Your work for Lady Marshbourne is done. That leaves Sir Percival."

"If I'm satisfied none of the family has a part in it, then I'll tell Uncle Percy so." Freddie didn't mention Sir Percival's unspoken suspicions. "Of course, I'll tell the police too."

"If you stumble on any evidence against one of the Tollarhithes, bring it straight to me. Don't do anything stupid and put yourself in danger. A murderer will kill again to protect himself, even if he's related to a baronet. Now, we might find out that Toby Glovins had enemies in Foxborough or other 'special friends,' but it's also possible that someone you know had good reason to want him dead."

The inspector seemed to have a specific person in mind. "Who?" Freddie asked.

"Look at that list of names you gave me, the

young people who were in the garden last night. Miss Amelia Marsh didn't join you until after sunset. The rest of you were together all afternoon, you and Captain Marsh, the two younger Marsh boys, Evelyn, Felix, and Phillip Tollarhithe, and all those Tollarhithe girls. Where was Miss Marsh at half-past six?"

Freddie felt a cold chill run up his spine. This wasn't a name he'd expected to hear. "She was in her room at her fiancé's home."

"Did you see her there?"

"No," he answered reluctantly.

5

When he met Kell and Phillip entering Foxgrove, Freddie gathered his two friends for a brief, private conference upstairs. It had become urgent that he make a list of suspects.

"You'll be the greatest help in figuring out who's the most likely person to have done this," he told them. "If Uncle Percy's right and one of the family is involved, then there's only a small group that's completely exempt from suspicion: Dotty and Bicky, Felix, and the girls, since we were all in the garden together. I think we can also exclude the Marsh ladies and other guests who are only here for the wedding. They had no reason to murder Toby Glovins. I doubt they even knew he existed. Now, who among the Tollarhithes might've wanted Toby dead?"

Kell considered the question. "Aside from Evelyn, I suppose Uncle Aubrey and Reg would be the ones most interested in seeing Toby gone for good. Their family reputation was at stake. I don't say they did it deliberately. They might've only wanted to stop Toby making a scene at the wedding and it went wrong."

"I can't see Uncle Aubrey even going so far as that," said Phillip. "He's the most mild-tempered man I know."

"Reg does seem more likely," Freddie agreed. "We know he was at the grove. He says that he followed Evelyn, but what if he actually went on ahead? He knew that the two would be meeting there, he admitted as much to me. He had only to find Toby waiting, kill him, then slip out of sight before Evelyn arrived."

"Would he do that to his brother, let poor Ev stumble over his friend's body?" Kell wondered. "He's a blighter, but that's a bit much."

"I don't see how he could avoid letting Ev in for it without giving himself away," said Freddie. "He's done his best to look out for Evelyn and protect him since. And it makes sense that if Uncle Percy suspects Reg, he'd want to shield him, his daughter's husband, father to his grandson."

"Do you think he knows it's Reg?"

"No. If he knew who'd killed Toby—if he were certain of it—I think he'd prefer to take care of it himself. He'd want the matter cleared up, and hushed up. He's afraid and he wants to find out if what he's afraid of is true."

"Have you considered it might actually be Uncle Percy?" asked Kell. "Family reputation means as much to him as Reg and Uncle Aubrey, if not more. He'd go to great lengths to protect it."

"It's possible," Freddie admitted. "I'm certain he knows more than he's told me about this business, but I don't think he's responsible for it. He wouldn't have asked me to investigate if he did."

"Maybe he had no choice," countered Kell. "Once he knew that Mother asked you to look into things, he might think it'd look less suspicious to help you than to stand in your way. That way, he knows precisely how much you know."

They both became aware that Phillip was staring at them and felt ashamed of themselves for their tactlessness. They were, after all, discussing his father.

"Father might commit murder for *me*," said Phillip, "but I don't think he'd do it for Ev. Besides, there are other people much more likely. Father says there's another boy who's gone missing. Could he be the murderer?"

"The butcher's apprentice? I don't know a thing about him, except that he's gone," said Freddie. "He might've killed Toby and then run away, or perhaps he saw something that made him a danger to Toby's killer, and he had to be silenced. I'd rather leave that end of the mystery to the police to solve. Uncle Percy's asked me to look into Toby's death because of the family, and that's where I mean to concentrate my attention."

"If Felix hadn't been with us, I'd say he might've wanted Toby out of the way," Phillip suggested.

"Felix?" asked Kell. "Why Felix?"

"Well, he's Evvy's best friend. Maybe he was jealous."

"Of Toby? But Felix likes girls."

"So he says, but I know Ev and Felix better than you do. They used to be quite close as schoolboys before this Toby came around. Even if he likes girls better, Felix must've been a little jealous when Ev found himself a new boyfriend, don't you think?"

"Jealous or not, it isn't possible. Felix was never out of our sight all afternoon." Kell paused, then said, "But Mellie wasn't. I don't like to think of it, but there it is."

Freddie nodded solemnly. He'd been waiting for Mellie's name to come up again, and hoping that it wouldn't. "We must consider her," he was forced to agree. "I just had a word with John Deffords. He's already taken note that we can't confirm where she was before she came out into the garden."

Kell was obviously not as pleased at Deffords's reappearance as Freddie had been. "'John'?" he repeated.

"It's his Christian name. Surely you didn't think it was Inspector."

"No, but when did the two of you become such chums?"

"When I was looking into Wilfrid's disappearance and he was investigating the murder of Daisy Putey. Our cases intersected."

Kell nodded. "You did seem on rather friendly terms. I wondered about it at the time."

"I think we are becoming friends," said Freddie. "I'd like us to be. A friend among the police will be of help to us in our line of business."

"Your line of business, old chap. Mine will be aeroplanes if I can get the bally thing off the ground. 'Til then, I'm simply helping you out for the fun of it. I'll stay out of the way of your police chum, if you don't mind. I'd rather keep Mellie out of his way too, if we can."

"So would I, but we have to look at everyone, like it or not. I learned that the last time. For that same reason, we ought to consider Aunt Theresa. I don't think she had any idea Toby existed before he was killed, but if she did, the last thing she would want is her daughter's wedding spoiled by scandal."

"Mellie's and Ev's wedding was spoiled just the same," Kell said. "If the murder didn't put an end to it, the show that little rotter put on for us all certainly did." He was very fond of Amelia and didn't like her being subjected to the sort of brutal public humiliation he'd witnessed this morning.

Freddie was also thinking of how stricken Amelia had looked. "Ev has behaved rottenly, but I promised her I'd do my best for him. We must learn where everyone else was between tea-time and sunset, when Evelyn left us to meet Toby. Kell, will you inquire about the ladies? Your mother will be happy to help. Phil, I want to know more about Reg. We know where he was, or at least where he says he was. Can you verify that? Perhaps Phaedra or Uncle Aubrey were with him before he followed Ev. And see if you can confirm whether or not Mellie was in her room."

Luncheon at Foxgrove was a more subdued meal than that morning's breakfast. The death of a young man that none of them knew well had been alarming; the cancelled wedding and the painful scene witnessed between Amelia and Evelyn was more personally distressing to the families of both. The food on the sideboard, cold meats, salads, and jellies meant for the cancelled festivities, were an additional reminder of what today should have been. No one wanted to talk about it; conversation between Sir Percival's family and their Marsh guests focused on whether or not they would attend the inquest that afternoon, until Theresa joined the table.

"Mellie's resting at last," she reported as she took her seat. "The poor girl's terribly distraught. She couldn't think of eating, but a tray ought to be sent up to Emily, who's been kind enough to sit with her and let me come down. Egeria dear, can you please see that

Mellie's things are brought over from Aubrey's house and put into my room? I won't have her staying another night under the same roof as Evelyn Tollarhithe."

"Evelyn's been cleared of suspicion," said Percival. "The police believe that he couldn't possibly have killed that boy."

"Evelyn's behaved like a beast to my daughter today. He mayn't be a murderer, but he's indisputably done that. We were all there to see it." Theresa stabbed her fork into her salad. "Well, he was quite right about one thing: Mellie's had a lucky escape. If I'd known what he was truly like, I would never have let her come here to him. Disgraceful, I call it. Can you imagine—he meant to marry Mellie and carry on with– with– well!"

"Evelyn told me that he broke with Toby before he became engaged to Mellie," said Freddie.

"Then why was he running off to meet that boy the night before his wedding?" asked Theresa. "Whatever his intentions, Evelyn's actions declare themselves beyond a doubt."

Piggy looked around the table at her brother and the young Marshes in wonderment and asked frankly, "Do all boys carry on like that?" Phillip wasn't the only Tollarhithe who believed in asking direct questions.

"Piggy!" her mother cried, shocked.

"Young girls shouldn't ask about such things," Diana chided. "You shouldn't know about them at all."

"Well, I don't know, but I want to," Piggy protested. "It's best to be honest. If I'm going to marry one day, I'd rather know what to expect. I don't mean to share my husband with anyone."

"Iphegenia Tollarhithe!" Egeria insisted. "That's quite enough."

"Did you hear any gossip about Evelyn and Toby Glovins before today?" Freddie asked. He'd been trying to think of a delicate way to broach the question, but since Piggy had brought the subject up already, this seemed like a good opportunity. "Did you know that they met in the grove?"

"This is hardly a fit conversation for the dining table," observed Diana.

"I don't see why we shouldn't answer," Percival supported Freddie. "I had heard something about it, yes."

"I knew Ev was friends with Toby Glovins. Everyone knew that," said Perdita. "We used to see Ev walk out into the meadow at evening, but I never guessed there was anything... wrong about it." Her face was pink.

"I did," said Piggy. "I mean, I guessed. After all that trouble about Phil, I couldn't help wondering."

Egeria gave her daughter another sharp look, but the struggle to maintain a standard of decorum had already been lost. "I certainly hadn't the least idea," she proclaimed. "Such unpleasant thoughts have never entered my head unbidden. We used not to acknowledge that such goings-on even existed. Must we speak of them openly? What is England coming to?"

"It's the modern age, Auntie," Kell answered. "Nothing's been the same since the war, and I hope it carries on this way."

After lunch, Freddie met with Sir Percival in the library. "I've spoken to Evelyn," he reported. "Phillip and Kell are assisting me, and we're trying to find out where everyone was when Toby was killed. You don't mind if I ask: Where were you before you joined us in the garden last night?"

Percival wasn't offended, but seemed amused by the question. "I was with Aubrey in his study at the Vixen. We were discussing Evelyn, as a matter of fact, and his unfortunate connection with Toby Glovins."

"Uncle Aubrey knew about it?"

"Oh, yes. We've both known for quite some time. The problem has troubled his father deeply, especially since Evelyn became engaged."

Interesting as this piece of information was, Freddie noted that both men's whereabouts were accounted for. "Have you thought," he tentatively put forward his theory, "that Reginald might be implicated?"

"Reginald?" Percival looked curious.

"He was there ahead of the rest of us, at Evelyn's side when we found them. You observed that too."

"Yes, I noticed."

"He says that he followed Evelyn out to the meadow to try and prevent him from seeing Toby again."

"But you doubt that?"

"I wonder," Freddie admitted, but didn't dare to go further until he knew what his uncle thought about it. Was Reg the one Percival suspected?

"I hadn't considered it, but you're right." Percival left the chair he'd been sitting in and began to pace. "I hope it isn't true. It would crush Phaedra. Poor Aubrey would be heartbroken."

He seemed sincerely disturbed at the idea of his son-in-law's guilt; Freddie was certain that Sir Percival hadn't considered it before. Reg wasn't the one he suspected. Then who was he thinking of?

Kell, meanwhile, went upstairs to see his mother. He tapped lightly on the door to Theresa's room, then pushed it open to find Emily sitting in a chair at the bedside. Amelia lay on the bed, one arm flung over her eyes. A luncheon tray had been left on a table outside the door and he brought it in.

"Aunt Theresa thought you'd be hungry," he said in a whisper. "There's enough for you too, Mellie," he added, not certain if his cousin were sleeping or awake.

"Thank you, Kell." Mellie lowered her arm and lifted her head from the pillow. "I couldn't..." But as she looked over the tray of salmon mousse, salad, gooseberry tartlets, and other dainties, she reconsidered. She sat up and took a tartlet. Emily also had something to eat.

"When you're done, Mother, I'd like to talk to you," Kell requested. "I want to ask a few questions, if you don't mind."

Emily smiled. "Is this part of Freddie's investigation?"

"If you're worried about troubling me, you can leave me alone," said Mellie. "I'll be all right by myself, Aunt Emily."

They went next door to Emily's room. "What would you like to know?" Emily asked as she sat down on the settee at the foot of her bed.

Kell sat down beside her. "Can you tell me where the ladies were yesterday afternoon after tea, particularly Phillip's mother, Aunt Diana, and Aunt Theresa?"

"But not Matilda nor me? Well, it makes no difference. We were in the drawing room, every one of us. All the ladies you've asked after and Felix's mother too. We never left after tea."

"No one left the drawing room?"

"No. We sat and talked until we heard the

commotion outside. Phillip told us what had happened."

The ladies were unlikely murderers, but Kell was relieved to hear that they could be excluded from suspicion. "What about Uncles Percival and Aubrey? Were they with you?"

Emily laughed. "Goodness, no! There are certain things that ladies simply can't speak of when gentlemen are present. It would only shock and embarrass them."

"What on earth did you talk about?" Kell wondered if he would regret asking the question, but he was curious.

"You, my dear," his mother told him. "You and Phillip. Egeria is very worried about her son, you know. She and Di have been discussing what to do about him. After you young people had gone out, they consulted me."

Kell grinned. His mother had missed the lunch conversation, where some of the ladies had been very frank in front of gentlemen. It also seemed that Phillip had been perfectly right about his mother worrying over 'the problem'; Egeria and Diana apparently had no qualms about the propriety of discussing these delicate subjects in the company of other ladies alone. "They wanted your advice?"

"They wanted to know what I meant to do with you. Diana says that there are some very good alienists and nerve specialists these days who can achieve remarkable results in cases like yours, but Egeria believes it's simply a matter of doing one's duty. She said that if you'd only behave, then Phillip would too."

"What did you tell her?"

"I said that I had no idea of sending you to a doctor if you didn't want to go. I also told them it'd do no good to push girls at Phillip if he isn't interested in looking at them. That didn't work when your father tried it. We can only be patient, and if in the end you never choose to marry..." She sighed. "It isn't an end to England, nor even to our families. I'm sure this sort of thing has happened many times before. In the old days, you would simply have lived your private life in secret whether you married or not."

"I'd be happy to live quietly, mind my own business, and not bother anyone," said Kell, "but as long as these beastly old laws pry into my private affairs, I don't have much choice. But I'm no coward. I won't lie and I won't be ashamed of myself." He'd never imagined having such a conversation with his mother, and yet, here they were. He asked her tentatively, "You're not ashamed of me, are you?"

"Oh, my darling, no! I might wish things were different, but I've never been sorry to call you my son, the only son I have. If only Egeria could see it in the same light."

When Phillip left Foxgrove, he went out through one of the garden doors and spotted Aubrey, Phaedra, and Reginald seated at a table on the Vixen's terrace. This seemed like a perfect opportunity to begin his assigned task.

"Hello!" he called out as he approached them. "Still having your lunch?"

"Just finishing. Why don't you join us?" offered Phaedra.

Even though he'd already had a good lunch, Phillip sat down to help himself and asked, "How's Ev?"

"Worse since he saw Mellie," Reginald reported, "and since Freddie Babington came to poke his nose into things that are none of his business."

"Freddie's only doing as Father asked," said Phillip.

"Perhaps, but he doesn't have to investigate *us*."

"Felix is with Evelyn now," said Aubrey. "I thought someone ought to stay by him. I'm afraid the poor lad might do himself a harm."

"He's only made a bad lot worse," said Phaedra. "I know he's distraught over the death of his friend, but he needn't have made a spectacle of himself."

Phillip was normally a firm believer in the effectiveness of direct questions, but he realized that this time he would have to be more circuitous if he wanted to find anything out. "It's a shame about the wedding," he began. "Everyone's expected Ev and Mellie to marry since they were children, and now it's come to nothing." He poured himself a glass of lemonade. "Mellie worked so hard on that dress of hers."

"It's a shame," Phaedra agreed.

"Felix was telling us about it," Phillip continued blithely. "The piece of old lace she had to sew on. It sounded rather complicated. You must've helped her a bit, Phee."

"No, Mellie wouldn't have anyone's help. She wanted to do the whole piece of work herself. She was shut up in her room all yesterday afternoon to try to finish in time. I hope she'll have the opportunity to wear it after all."

"You think the marriage will go on, after the way Evvy behaved to her?"

"I know he's been a fool, but she's a sweet, understanding girl. She'd forgive him. I'd daresay she'd even forgive his friendship with that awful Toby, especially now that Toby's dead."

"It's only a matter of time before the murderer is caught," said Reg. "If Uncle Percy's private investigator doesn't find him, the police will."

"Who do you think did it?" Phillip asked.

Reg regarded him suspiciously. "You're not spying for Freddie, are you?"

"I was only wondering," Phillip answered with an air of innocence. "Isn't that just what everyone's wondering about? Somebody stabbed Toby."

"Yes, but it's nothing to do with us," Phaedra insisted. "He was Evelyn's friend and was found on Father's property, but that doesn't mean that we're involved. It must've been a wandering tramp or a farm lad he had a quarrel with who killed him, or someone of the sort."

"You don't think it's one of the family?"

"Phillip!" his sister exclaimed. "How can you think such a thing?"

"I do," Aubrey said quietly. "It wouldn't surprise me to find that Archibald's behind this."

The young people stared at him. "Great-Uncle Archibald?" Reginald repeated. "Why? He didn't even know Toby Glovins, did he?"

"No," Aubrey admitted, "but you don't know what that old wretch is capable of."

"Really, Uncle Aubrey," Phaedra murmured reprovingly, and sounded so exactly like their mother that Phillip had to grin.

"My apologies, my dear," Aubrey bowed his head, rebuked. "You're quite right. I've said more than I should. If you'll excuse me, I'll go and see how Evelyn is doing. We mustn't leave young Felix to bear all our responsibilities." He went into the house.

"I never heard Uncle Aubrey speak like that before about anyone," Phillip said in astonishment.

"What makes him think that old Archibald's had a part in this?"

"I couldn't say," Reg replied. "Oh, I know Uncle Archibald talks rather fierce sometimes, but he's harmless. He must be over eighty. Father's never liked him. He doesn't even like to be near the old gent if he can help it."

Phillip nodded. He remembered that his father and Uncle Aubrey had quarreled with the old man not long after the death of the last baronet, Sir Alvin; he'd only been a small boy at the time. Archibald had gone away to live on the other side of Norwich, but he seemed to have been restored to the family since. "Is Great-Uncle Archibald living here now? Not at the Vixen, I mean. In Foxborough."

"No," said Phaedra. "He only came for the wedding."

"He came for our wedding too," Reginald added. "He's always taken an interest in us, Ev and the girls and me, though I don't understand why. I remember once when I was very small, he came to visit and asked to see me. Mother had me brought down from the nursery. I wasn't more than three or four years old. Alma was just a baby, and Ev and Isolde hadn't even been born. Old Uncle Archibald looked me over and seemed pleased. He told Mother what a fine looking boy I was. Then he said to me, 'You have me to thank. You wouldn't have been born at all if it weren't for me.'"

"What could he mean by that?" Phillip asked. "It sounds very odd." Should he tell Freddie about it?

"I've no idea. Uncle Archibald's a peculiar old man," said Reginald. "All the same, I don't think what Father's said about him can be true." He and Phaedra exchanged a glance. "No," they agreed.

"It's this terrible situation preying on Uncle Aubrey's mind," said Phaedra. "Worrying about Ev has given him some strange ideas."

Reginald went indoors after his father. The nurse had brought the baby outdoors after his bottle; instead of placing him in his bassinet, Phaedra insisted that Phillip hold him. He bounced the baby on his knee, until she warned him, "Careful, Phil, don't shake him so much. He'll make a mess of your shirt."

Phillip brought little Peveril to his shoulder and cradled him gingerly.

"That's right," Phaedra told him. "Give his back a pat or two."

He did so, terrified that the baby would spit up on him.

"There," his sister said approvingly. "You really are very good with babies. Reg looks frightened to death every time he holds Peveril. He's so afraid he'll drop him on his head, even though he can hold the baby quite securely in the crook of his left arm. I expect you'll be a wonderful father one day."

Reluctantly, Phillip had to admit that the idea had its appeal.

Phaedra watched his face and said, "I've heard that you won't meet Auntie Di's niece."

"I don't mind meeting the girl," Phillip replied. "When she's here, I'll see her and I'll be as nice as you please, but I won't marry her. I don't even know her."

"Mother and Father were an arranged match and they've done very well together. Uncle Aubrey and Aunt Evangeline were matched too." She paused, then asked, "Is it because of Kell that you won't think of it?"

"Isn't that reason enough?" Phillip braced

himself for an argument. Phaedra was ten years his senior and could be as intimidating as his parents.

Phaedra answered with surprising sympathy, "I do understand, Phil. Mother doesn't. She thinks it's all schoolboy naughtiness, but I've watched you two together since you were small. You've always looked up to Kell. You'd do whatever he asked."

"You think he's led me astray?"

"No, but I think you're old enough to decide for yourself. You can't let Kell Marsh choose for you all your life."

"I have decided," Phillip insisted, "only nobody likes my choice. You ought to be pleased if I don't marry, Phee. Little Pev can be my heir." He patted the baby, who slept against his shoulder. "He'll make a good twelfth baronet if he takes after you. You're the sensible one, not like the rest of us."

Phaedra laughed, and Phillip hoped he'd distracted her. Perhaps they wouldn't have to go on with this serious conversation about his private life after all.

"You'd be a better baronet than me," he said. "It should go to you."

If Phaedra thought so too—and Phillip knew she did—she had the grace not to say so. "A daughter can't inherit," she answered. "It has to be a son. As much as I'd like my son to be your heir, Phil, you ought to have one of your own. No one's suggesting that you marry tomorrow or even next year, only think about the future, will you, for the family's sake?"

The conversation ended mercifully at this point when Felix came out onto the terrace. At Phaedra's invitation, he took a sandwich, but didn't sit down with them. "Mother and Father must be wondering what's happened to me," he said. "How's Freddie's investigation coming along, Phil? Find anything yet?"

"I wouldn't know," Phillip responded. He felt his sister's eyes upon him.

"When you see him, tell him I wish him the best of luck. The sooner this murder is solved, the better for all of us."

After Felix had gone, Phaedra turned to Phillip. "You are helping Freddie, aren't you?"

Phillip didn't answer immediately; he could never get a lie past his eldest sister.

His embarrassed silence was enough for Phaedra to divine the truth. "I wondered about the questions you were asking," she said. "You wanted to find out what we knew. Did he send you here to interrogate us?"

Phillip nodded abashedly. "Freddie didn't think you'd talk to him," he confessed. "Well, not you, Phee, but Reg. You heard how he was speaking of Freddie's visit this morning."

"Yes. I don't know what Freddie said to him, but I can see that Reg is afraid that Freddie suspects him. Will you tell me why? Is it because Reg didn't approve of Evelyn's friendship with that boy? But that's nonsense. None of us did."

"Didn't you?"

"I tried to take no notice of it," Phaedra replied. "Mother says there are things a lady simply doesn't acknowledge, and it was none of my business, really." She regarded her brother. "Does Freddie suspect Reg? For goodness sake, why?"

"Reg was there with Evvy when we found Toby's body," Phillip explained. "He told Freddie that he sat here on the terrace and waited for Ev to leave, then followed him. We... ah, wondered if he could've gone out to the meadow earlier."

"Is that all?" Phaedra looked relieved. "As a matter of fact, Reg did sit here on the terrace while you were all down in the garden. I sat with him until the sun went down and it began to be chilly."

"When did you go?" Phillip asked her eagerly. "Was it long before sunset?"

"No, it was just at dusk. Seven o'clock." She smiled. "Reg couldn't have gone out earlier. He can't be suspected. Tell Freddie that."

Phillip left Phaedra not long afterwards. As he passed Aubrey's study, which opened onto the terrace, the French window swung slightly open.

"Ah, Phil." Aubrey stood just within, waiting for him. "Come in for a moment, please?"

Phillip went inside. His uncle's study was smaller and less impressive than his father's, and Phillip had always found it more pleasant. He'd spent many happy hours of his boyhood here with his uncle when he was hiding from his own parents. No one had called him into this room for a scolding. The old slant-top desk was still before the windows, and his old favorite books full of historical engravings and colored plates of far-away lands remained on the shelves. The mantelpiece was decorated with hand-carved wooden sculptures, some familiar, some new. This was Aubrey's hobby. Phillip and his sisters had received many presents over the years of cleverly designed toys and elaborate little puzzle boxes that came apart to reveal hidden compartments; Phillip had several of them in his bedroom. Aubrey's latest, unfinished piece of handiwork and a bone-handled knife sat on his work-table by the fire, next to his worn and comfortable armchair; wood shavings were scattered on the hearth.

"What is it, Uncle Aubrey?" Phillip asked.

"You are investigating this murder with Freddie, aren't you?"

Phillip was dismayed. He'd deceived no one with his attempts at subterfuge. "Well, yes," he admitted.

Aubrey sighed. "You must do what you have to, but I've been thinking that it might be best to leave this matter alone. Bury poor Toby and let him rest. Looking into his death is only going to bring up things that are better forgotten. It'll be worse for us all in the end. It's turning ugly already; Evelyn and Amelia's happiness ruined, and the family starting to wonder if he wasn't murdered by one of us. They'll say they wouldn't dream of thinking it, but think it they will."

"You said you thought Great-Uncle Archibald was behind it," said Phillip. Since subtlety hadn't worked, he might as well be direct. "Why?"

His uncle seemed somewhat flustered by the abrupt question. "I said too much, Phil. It was unpardonable of me to make an accusation like that without proof. I'd better have kept my mouth shut. I hope you won't take too much account of it. You won't repeat it, will you?"

Even if he didn't understand, Phillip was fond enough of his uncle to say, "I won't. Unless it turns out to be important, I won't."

"It's not important. Thank you. You're a good lad." Aubrey gave him an approving pat on the shoulder. "I've always said so."

"Even when Father didn't."

Aubrey laughed. "I know he and your mother have been giving you a difficult time lately, Phil, but I have to tell you that I'm proud of the way you've stood up for yourself against their wishes. Don't give in, not if it isn't what you want."

This unexpected encouragement was more surprising than anything else Phillip had heard from his uncle that day, and more baffling.

6

The inquest was held that afternoon at the Foxborough parish hall. A few reporters, attracted by the combined newsworthy elements of a dead body, a baronet's family, and a cancelled society wedding, had come up from London, but they heard little of the salacious details they were hoping for.

Mr. Thornton testified that he'd been summoned at 7:25 via telephone and arrived at 7:48 to view the body of a young man who had apparently been stabbed in the chest in the meadow behind Foxgrove. The young man was identified to him by Sir Percival Tollarhithe as Tobias Anthony Glovins of Foxborough. This identification was later confirmed by Christopher Glovins, Toby's father. Thornton had noticed immediately that no knife was in the wound; he described the efforts made by the police to locate it. The weapon hadn't yet been found and it was presumed that whoever stabbed Toby had taken it away with him.

Dr. Preston presented his medical evidence. He'd examined the body of Tobias Glovins on the site at approximately 7:50. Given the temperature of the body, no advancement of rigor, and other factors, he could say that the young man had died just over an hour before he'd arrived, 6:30 to 6:40 according to his best estimate. He'd conducted a full autopsy the following morning and described the mortal wound to the heart, inflicted by a short-bladed knife. He then added a piece of information Freddie hadn't heard before: the blade had entered at an unusually low and oblique angle. If the assailant had struck while facing his victim, he must have used his left hand. The right hand could only have been used if he'd come upon his victim from behind and reached around his chest. In answer to a question from the coroner, the doctor acknowledged that the angle of the wound was not inconsistent with a self-inflicted blow, but if that were the case, what had happened to the weapon?

Evelyn was called up next. Mildly sedated, he was sufficiently composed to give coherent evidence about how he'd discovered his friend's body. He stated that he'd known Toby Glovins for three years, that he'd gone out that evening to meet Toby in the meadow, and had found Toby dead. He spoke so matter-of-factly that his statement failed to rouse the bored reporters' curiosity.

Reginald testified that he'd been walking along the stream at the bottom of the garden around 7 pm when he'd seen his brother cross the bridge into the meadow. He had heard his brother scream less than a minute later and hastened to the grove to find Evelyn kneeling beside Toby's body. He'd observed no knife in the vicinity. His brother had no knife with him.

Sir Percival had asked Freddie and Kell to speak for the group who'd been in the garden that night since they were older than most of the other witnesses, had seen service, and would make a good impression on the coroner. Freddie suspected that Percival also wished to avoid placing his own children and nieces on the stand. Both in turn affirmed that Evelyn had left them at sunset and not more than ten minutes had passed before they heard him scream. Felix testified to finding the knife Evelyn had used to cut flowers in the grass near the pavilion after the murder. Sir Percival's testimony emphasized the brief amount of time between Evelyn's departure and the discovery of the body by himself and the young people. Phillip was there but wasn't called to testify; Amelia and the Tollarhithe girls weren't present, but Sir Percival made it clear that these additional witnesses could be produced to verify Evelyn's whereabouts at the time of the murder if necessary.

The police had no evidence to offer. The missing apprentice was not mentioned.

The coroner called for the inquest to reconvene in one week pending further evidence, and authorized the release of the body to Christopher Glovins for funeral arrangements. Mr. Glovins was too distraught by his son's death to attend the inquest, but the coroner expressed his sympathies for the grieving father and family.

Freddie, Kell, and Phillip had no time to discuss their progress before the inquest, but the three crossed Foxborough's High Street and met in the St. Barnabas churchyard immediately afterwards to put together all they'd learned concerning the whereabouts of the Tollarhithes and Marshes.

"Everyone's accounted for, except Mellie," Freddie concluded glumly.

"One of them might be lying," Kell concluded. "Uncles Aubrey and Percy are great friends. If Uncle Percy thought Aubrey had killed Toby, he'd say they were both in Aubrey's study when he hadn't been there or knew that Aubrey wasn't. Phaedra would lie to say she was with Reg if it saved him."

"I hate this kind of talk," said Phillip from his perch on a mossy tombstone. "I don't like you calling them liars. Phee's never told a lie in her life. I don't think she would, even for Reg."

"I'm sorry, Phil, but that's the way we must look at it if we're to conduct this investigation properly. Isn't that right, Freddie?" Kell answered. "It's no good to say that somebody or other can't have committed a murder. We have to ask, 'What if they did?' We have to consider everyone. That doesn't mean we believe it's true."

"It's what Billy taught me. He'd say the same this time," Freddie agreed.

"It'd be easy for him to say it," Phillip retorted. "He's never had to suspect his own family."

"Not suspect," said Kell, "only consider."

Freddie added, "Your father does believe one of the Tollarhithes is involved."

"Just because Father believes it doesn't mean it's so," Phillip responded defensively. "He might be wrong. A baronet can be wrong, you know. Besides, if one of the family killed Toby, then it must've been to shut him up. They didn't want him to cause a scandal. But if that's what they meant to do, it didn't work. Toby dead makes a much worse scandal than anything he might've said about Evvy when he was alive. Nobody who wanted to kill Toby to keep him quiet would've done it the way they did."

"Maybe they didn't think he'd be found right away," said Kell.

"No," Freddie said, "Phil's right. Whoever went to the grove that evening knew they'd find Toby there and must've known why. It was the place where Evelyn and Toby always met. That was no secret, the whole family knew about it. Whoever killed Toby must've realized that Evelyn would find his friend's body. Once that happened, events would unfold just as they have. The police would be summoned. Questions would be asked. The truth would come out. There was no way to avoid it."

"They might not have intended murder," Kell suggested. "I've said so before, and I like that idea much better. Anyone might've gone there only meaning to chase Toby off before Evelyn arrived."

"If that's so, why bring a knife?" asked Freddie.

"To threaten him, perhaps. Or they might've simply had it with them. The police are looking for a small, sharp knife, the sort anybody might keep at hand for cutting string or whittling a bit of wood."

Phillip, who had been glancing from one to the other, following their discussion, suddenly went so pale that his freckles stood out. Freddie and Kell didn't notice.

"Each of us had a pocket-knife with us yesterday when we were cutting flowers and trimming the stems for the garlands," Kell continued. "It's a good thing Ev left his behind. It'd be much worse for him if he'd still had it with him when he found Toby."

"There's something in what you say," Freddie agreed. "Pocket-knives don't draw much attention. Anyone might carry one. The doctor said that Toby was probably stabbed from the front by a left-handed person. If that's so, whoever wielded the knife stood directly before him. Did he see it? If he was being threatened by it, certainly."

"Reg seems the sort of blustering ass most likely to try such a tactic, but he can't have struck a left-handed blow. He doesn't have one anymore."

"The only way Reg could've attacked Toby is from behind. He'd put what remains of his left arm around Toby's neck to hold him while he wielded the knife in his right hand. He's got enough of his arm left to do that, and some strength in it."

"But Toby would surely have struggled."

"That's another thing that's been puzzling me. Mr. Thornton says there were signs of a struggle. We mightn't have heard that, but we would've heard Toby cry out for help, just as we heard Evelyn when he screamed. But he didn't scream. Why not?"

"He didn't realize he was in danger for his life?" Kell guessed. "He wasn't truly afraid until it was too late? Don't forgot, Freddie, it was still quite light at that time. Hard to sneak up on a chap in a meadow where the grass is barely knee-deep. He probably saw whoever it was coming toward the grove."

"A friend then," said Freddie. "At least, someone he didn't believe would do him harm. Kell, we must find out if everyone was where they say they were. Can you and Phil find out if anyone saw Phaedra with Reg on the terrace? We were sitting with our backs to the Vixen, but the girls or Felix might've seen them. I'll talk to Uncle Percival. If I press him about Uncle Aubrey, he might admit that that's who he's worried about."

"We've all seen Uncle Aubrey work at his wood-carving. He holds a knife left-handed–"

Phillip let out a sharp yelp.

Kell turned to him. "What's the matter with you?"

"I told you, I don't like this. It's my family you're talking about."

Kell sat down beside him and put an arm around him. "Hush, Phil. Hush. We won't go on about it." He glanced up at Freddie. "Leave us alone, will you? There's been enough talk of murder for today."

As he left his friends in the churchyard, Freddie saw that Deffords, who had also attended the inquest, was lingering outside the parish hall. Waiting to talk to him?

"Are you returning to Weymondham tonight?" he called out.

Deffords shook his head. "My men've gone back with their photographs and dabs, but Mr. Thornton's asked me to dinner. I'm staying at The Grapes." This was an old coaching inn farther down the High Street. "Do you have time for a pint?"

"Yes, of course. I've no reason to hurry back." Kell was accompanying Phillip up the street in the opposite direction, toward the Foxgrove Park gates. Before they went in, Kell looked over his shoulder and met Freddie's eyes; he wasn't pleased to see Freddie conferring with the inspector. "Let's go."

On their way to the inn, Deffords said, "I talked to the people in the smaller house this afternoon, Mr. Aubrey Tollarhithe and his elder son, the one with one arm..." Since he was still sorting out the numerous Tollarhithes, he had to consult his notes. "That's Reginald, and his wife. Sir Percival told them to answer my questions. He's been more helpful than I expected, probably because of you. I wanted to find out if they knew Toby Glovins and where they were yesterday afternoon before sunset. The younger Mr. Tollarhithe seemed put out, as if he'd had enough of answering questions already."

Freddie chuckled. "We've been going around and asking everyone in the family. I was rather hard on Reg this morning. I suspected him for a while, but now I'm not so sure."

"His wife swears she was with him until sunset," said Deffords. His tone suggested that he'd heard innumerable wives swearing to their husbands' whereabouts regardless of the truth.

"She told Phil the same thing and he believes her. All the same, I've asked Kell to see if he can confirm it." Some reporters were lingering in The Grapes public room after the inquest. Rather than be overheard, Freddie and the inspector went into the bar-parlor; no one else was there.

After they'd settled down with their drinks, Freddie decided to confide, "When you talked to Uncle Percy, did he leave you with the impression that he was afraid for some member of his family in particular?"

"The only person I can see he's trying to protect is Evelyn. At the inquest, he made it as plain as he could to the jury and reporters that his nephew couldn't have killed that boy. I think he's more afraid of a scandal than an arrest for murder. You can tell him there's no reason for it, by the way. My sergeant went through Toby Glovin's things. He found a few notes signed E, arranging meetings in that grove or at a local pub. Nothing more incriminating. Nothing to suggest Toby had other friends in the same way, or enemies for that matter. The father was too upset to give us anything useful. He holds the Tollarhithes responsible for his son's death, but doesn't accuse any of them specifically."

"Anyone else?" Freddie couldn't help asking, "You haven't talked to Mellie, have you?"

"Miss Marsh? No, she's at Foxgrove and I haven't been there yet. Sir Percival's arranged for me to interview his household and guests in the morning." He regarded Freddie. "Have you found out where she was? The family at the Vixen's Den think she was up in her room, but they admit they never saw her after tea."

Freddie confirmed that this was what Phillip had learned as well. "I can't believe Mellie would do such a thing."

"I don't have any evidence against her, but as long as she has no alibi, she has to be considered a suspect. You can't deny that. She was in love with Evelyn Tollarhithe, wasn't she? They were going to be married today. He was running around with Toby Glovins. I've seen plenty of women who've done worse over less. You thought she'd killed that other cousin of yours, Bertram Marsh."

"Yes, but I was wrong, you know I was. Besides, if she did strike Bertie, it was in her own defense. That's quite different from stabbing someone in cold blood."

"Is she left-handed?"

"I really hadn't noticed."

Deffords watched Freddie carefully as he asked, "Is she the one you're trying to protect this time, Freddie? I thought it was Evelyn."

"Evelyn's in little danger. Mellie..." Freddie sighed. "It'll take a great deal to convince me she's a murderess."

"I've never had a case that involved my own family," Deffords said after he finished his beer. "I don't have the hundreds of uncles, aunts, and cousins that you do. I can do my job without getting tangled up emotionally, but you get into these investigations to help the people you're closest to. You can't be impartial about them." He paused before he added, "I didn't realize you were sweet on this one girl."

"Mellie? Nonsense." Freddie rejected the idea. "I care for her, of course, but not in that way. She wouldn't even look at me."

It was dusk by the time Freddie returned to Foxgrove Park. At this same hour yesterday, they'd found Toby dead. Instead of entering the house, he walked a little way down the drive toward the Vixen and let himself in through a latched iron gate in the garden wall. He wasn't ready to face anybody yet.

The garden was quiet, seemingly abandoned, but as he wandered the shrubbery, he heard the sound of someone sobbing. Freddie traced the sound to the pavilion. The decorative lanterns that had been hung up around the lawn remained unlit, but there was enough light cast from the Vixen's windows for him to see Amelia weeping in the bower they'd made for her.

"Mellie?"

She lifted her face from her handkerchief. "Freddie?"

"Are you all right?"

"I'm fine... as well as can be expected. I had to get away. Everyone means well, but I can't bear to hear one more person tell me how lucky I am to be free of Evvy. I don't *feel* lucky! I'm sorry about the flowers," she added nonsensically. "You worked so hard on this silly bower and now it'll have to come down before they wilt and turn brown."

Freddie ventured a few steps closer. "Do you want me to leave you alone?"

"No," Mellie answered after a moment. "Since you're here, you might as well stay." She patted the wooden bench as an invitation to join her. "Are you still investigating?"

"Yes," he said as he sat down.

"You needn't continue on my account. You've done what I asked you to. I'm glad that Evvy won't be arrested, even if..." She took a deep breath and said deliberately, "even if we won't be married after all. I've loved Evelyn since I was six years old, Freddie. I never wanted anyone else. I thought he felt the same about me."

"I think," Freddie told her, "that if Evvy doesn't have the decency to apologize for the way he's treated you and beg you to take him back, he's a greater fool than I already believe he is."

Amelia laughed. "Oh, he's a great fool! After the things he said this morning, it's hopeless."

"Did you know about Evelyn and Toby before that?"

"No. I wouldn't have wanted him to marry me if I'd thought there was someone else. I wouldn't have kept him to his promise. It wouldn't have been much of a promise, would it, if he were still meeting his boyfriend in secret?"

"But Toby's gone now." In spite of himself, Freddie couldn't help thinking of what Deffords had said. No one could verify that Mellie had been in her room. She could easily have left the Vixen without being seen. She had more than enough reason for wanting to be rid of Toby: he was her rival. He had no intention of letting her be happy with Evelyn; he'd threatened to spoil their wedding.

Mellie was clutching her handkerchief in her left hand, and Freddie suddenly recalled how the governess who taught her to write had often switched the pen to her right hand until Mellie learned to hold it properly. Did people who preferred the left revert in moments of crisis?

It was too dark within the bower for Amelia to see his face, but she must guess his thoughts. Drawing away from him, she said, "Don't you dare think it, Freddie Babington. It was bad enough you suspected me of committing murder once, I won't stand for it again. Must I be careful of every word I say to you?

Are you offering a friend's sympathy, or this is an interrogation?"

"I'm sorry," Freddie said, immediately ashamed of himself. "It was meant to be one, but turned into the other. I didn't plan it, please, Mellie, you must believe that. The worst part of these investigations is that you have to consider everyone as a possible suspect, even the people dearest to you. You do suspect them, like it or not. I am sorry."

Amelia accepted this. "No, I didn't know," she said firmly. "I'd met Toby. Evelyn introduced us when I first came here, but he hardly ever spoke to me. I wondered if he might be jealous because Evvy didn't have much time for his old friends, but I never thought... I mean, even if it crossed my mind that he and Evvy were more than friends, I assumed that it was over and done with as far as Evvy was concerned. Most boys grow out of that sort of thing once they're out of school, don't they?"

"You know about that?" Freddie asked.

"I'm not so innocent, Freddie! Do you imagine anyone who's grown up in the same house as Kell Marsh can be ignorant of what goes on?" She crumpled her handkerchief between her hands as she confessed, "When I came here in the spring, I thought that Evelyn and I might, well, that we might go on ahead of the wedding night. That's not unheard of when you're about to be married," she explained quickly. "In these modern days, some of my friends have told the most shocking stories about what they've been up to. I thought that as long as we were both living in his father's house and had only a few weeks 'til the wedding, we needn't be old-fashioned and wait. I let Evvy understand that I was willing, if he wanted to." She laughed again. "Evvy didn't want to. He said we ought to wait. I thought he was considering my reputation or my maidenly virtue or some such nonsense. I know better now."

It was embarrassing to listen to such extremely personal confidences, but Freddie had learned enough about girls to realize that even the nice ones had these natural desires. Evelyn truly was an enormous fool.

Amelia turned to him suddenly. "Have you ever been in love, Freddie?" she asked.

"I think I might be," he confessed. "At least, I've only just realized how very dear someone is to me."

Amelia was quiet for a long while; he could see the glint of her eyes in the darkness as she regarded him. At last, she said, "You're very sweet, Freddie. I never realized..." She kissed him.

After pressing her lips to his for a few seconds, she stopped.

"Oh, I..." she said. "I'm sorry. I..." and she burst into tears.

What else could he do, but put his arms around her and hold her while she sobbed?

7

They were still holding each other when they heard Theresa calling her daughter's name from the Foxgrove terrace.

Mellie withdrew quickly from Freddie's arms. "Mother must be frantic," she said as she dabbed her face. "I'd better go and tell her I'm fine and make myself presentable for dinner. I must look a fright." She darted away before Freddie could say anything.

He followed her into the house and went upstairs to his own room. Kell was reclining on the bed and smoking a cigarette.

"Where's Phil?" Freddie asked.

"Having a nap before dinner," answered Kell. "It's been a thoroughly miserable day for all of us."

"Did he tell you what upset him?"

"No," Kell said shortly. "Asking only made it worse. Phil can be a thoughtless little blighter but he's quite sensitive when it strikes him. It must've struck him just when we were talking about which person in his family might be a murderer."

"We've all had to face suspecting our dearest relatives," Freddie said. He'd spent more than one bad night over that himself, and was faced with another in the near future. "None of us likes it."

"Yes, but Phil's closer to everyone this time and it isn't a game for him anymore. I think he's afraid." He looked up at Freddie. "Do you suppose he's learned something about one of them, somebody he truly cares for—Phee or Uncle Aubrey—and he doesn't want to tell us? You'd think he'd at least tell *me*."

Freddie had to smile; he'd said something very like it once. "You've kept secrets yourself, Kell, when it might've got you hanged," he reminded his cousin.

"That was different. I was protecting Mellie." Kell looked over him. "Where've you been, Freddie? Not talking to your inspector chum all this time."

"I've been in the garden, talking to Mellie as a matter of fact. She's in need of protection now too."

"You didn't tell her she's suspected?"

"Not by the police, no. I didn't dare." He saw Kell's eyes flicker to the tear-dampened patch on his shirt. "I didn't have a handkerchief with me. I gave mine to Evelyn earlier today. When she started crying, I didn't know what to do. Kell," he ventured, "have you ever been kissed by a girl?"

"Once or twice, though of course it's not my usual..." Kell, who had been leaning back propped on one elbow, sat upright. "Mellie?"

Freddie nodded.

"I suppose it was only a matter of time before some girl threw herself at you," Kell said in a contemplative tone. "I'm surprised it should be Mellie. Before or after she cried?"

"Before. Just before."

"Your intentions had better be honorable, Mr. Babington."

"Don't tease, Kell. You know she's in love with someone else."

"A boy who's been beastly to her. Ev's behaved like a swine. He couldn't be honest with either her or Toby. Serve him right if Mellie has nothing more to do with him. She'd be better off with you. Why don't you marry her, Freddie? You'd make a good husband. You're sweet, sympathetic, handsome."

"Not like you, old thing."

"You'll do." Kell said with a tone of critical appraisal. "You're too pale, but you've got a sensitive look that girls find attractive. Remarkable eyes, and a good nose in profile. When you let your curls grow long in front, you look like a Romantic poet in a frontispiece. More Keats, I'd say, than Byron or Shelley, a nice, safe poet that mothers would like their daughters to meet. If Aunt Theresa thought you'd propose to Mellie, she'd happily give Evelyn the push."

Freddie laughed nervously. "You're joking, Kell. You know my health–"

"What about it? Any young man with most of his arms and legs who hasn't gone off his head from shellshock is considered a catch these days. You're more fit than most, only a bit singed 'round the edges, not a dope fiend, and not entirely loopy."

"Not entirely," Freddie agreed. "All the same, it'd be dashed hard for a girl to put up with blood-curdling screams in the middle of the night. Mellie's been through enough without being asked to play nurse for me."

Kell's mouth dropped open, then he laughed in amazement. "Freddie, are you actually thinking about it?"

"Shut up, Kell."

He knew that Kell was only teasing, but he *was* seriously considering it.

Was he in love with her? He'd never considered the possibility before today. He'd denied it when both John Deffords and Kell had suggested it, and yet...

He was fonder of Mellie than any other girl. They'd grown up together in the Marsh Hall nursery and he would've said that she was as dear to him as a sister. He'd taken up this investigation primarily for her sake; in spite of the requests of his aunt and uncle, he wouldn't have agreed to undertake it if Mellie hadn't asked as well. He'd never resented her long-planned marriage to Evelyn. He had always wished them well and wouldn't have wanted their wedding to be postponed under such conspicuous circumstances. The additional humiliation of being rejected by her prospective bridegroom in the sight of both their families made it all the more terrible for Mellie. Freddie couldn't help feeling great compassion for her, and Deffords' suspicions had roused a surprisingly strong sense of protectiveness.

When he'd sat beside her in the bower, he'd only meant to comfort her, but even before that unexpected kiss had sent him into confusion, he'd begun to believe that his affection for her wasn't quite brotherly after all.

He'd never considered marriage for himself, but most of his relatives would say that he was of an age to think about it. He wasn't the great catch that Kell claimed he was. Mellie wasn't in love with him; he was well aware of that. But perhaps he could offer her an escape from this disaster. Why not ask, once she'd been given a little time to recover from Evelyn's rejection?

If he hesitated, it was for the same reason he urged his manservant Billy to marry. It was too much to ask to any healthy young person to devote their life to the care of a semi-invalid.

Dinner that night was an informal, family gathering. Freddie washed up but didn't bother to dress in evening clothes. When the first gong rang, announcing dinner in fifteen minutes, he went downstairs.

"Freddie?"

Mellie stood at the foot of the stairs. She had put on a fresh dress and powdered her nose. Except for the pinkish, tender skin around her eyes, she showed no signs of having wept.

"I wanted to talk to you," she said. "I thought we ought to, after what happened earlier."

"I've been… ah, thinking about that too," Freddie answered. "There's something I want to say to you as well."

To avoid being interrupted by the others assembling for dinner, they went into one of the unoccupied rooms overlooking the front drive. Mellie switched on a light. "I wanted to apologize. It was awfully silly of me, flinging myself at you and sobbing like an hysterical child." She spoke in a brisk, artificial tone that told him she'd rehearsed what she meant to say to him. "You were trying to be kind, and I made a fool of myself. I hope you didn't take it the wrong way. I don't want things to become awkward between us."

"I don't either, Mellie. You know I'm very fond of you."

"Good. I'm glad. What were you going to say, Freddie? It's not... it's not about Toby, is it?" The offhand pose she'd taken up faltered. "You aren't still afraid that I killed him?"

"No, of course not!"

"What about the police?"

"They'll suspect you," Freddie admitted reluctantly. "You did have a motive, you must see that. They can't overlook it. But if you've done nothing wrong then you've nothing to fear from them. I'll do what I can to look after you as far as the police are concerned. This business has been beastly enough for you without someone to stand beside you during the worst. But that's not why I wanted to talk to you." He plunged forward. "My manservant Bill, you know him?"

"Yes, certainly I remember Billy Watkins." She looked baffled. "He's been with you since you were boys."

"Well, he's thinking of... ah... marrying. I'd planned to do over the servants' rooms at the back of my flat in London to make them suitable for a couple, but lately I've been thinking that a flat meant for a bachelor and one manservant won't do anymore. I might take a larger flat. I also expect to come into some property one day, my Uncle Hilliard's house near Cambridge and Aunt Dora's in Abbotshill. Abbot House would be too large for me if I lived alone, but if I were to have a family..." He felt as if he were blathering incoherently, but as he spoke of families, Mellie's look of puzzlement faded and she began to regard him with fresh interest.

"I've always thought Abbot House one of the loveliest little houses in Suffolk," she said. Only someone who had grown up at the enormous Marsh Hall would call his aunt's Georgian manor 'little.'

"After we- ah, met earlier this evening, I had an idea. Perhaps a ridiculous idea. You must tell me if it is or not. I thought that if Evelyn were fool enough to throw you over and you'd rather not go home after all that's happened here, I'd like to offer you another place to go. Another home. Mine. A flat in London isn't quite what you were hoping to have with Evelyn, but it's what I have to give." He held up his hand. "Before you answer, there's something else you ought to know. I'm not well—I haven't been since I came home." He felt he had to be honest.

"I know that you were burned." Her gaze flickered to his scarred hand, then down over his body. "How... bad it is?"

"I'll always have scars, but at least my leg is better. That's not the trouble. I have nightmares about it, you see, that I'm trapped in that burning ruin."

She nodded. "When you were last at Marsh Hall, you woke everyone up one night."

"It happens when I'm disturbed or thinking too hard," Freddie explained. "Something goes wrong inside my head. There's a buzzing sound and the same thoughts go 'round and 'round like a needle stuck on a phonograph recording 'til I end up in a bad state. Not as bad as some poor chaps with shellshock, but I don't know if it will go away in time. There's a possibility that I may never be entirely well. I thought it was important for you to know what you'd have to put up with."

"I see." Tears glittered in Amelia's eyes. Freddie was certain that this information had frightened her off, but to his surprise, she took his hand. Her voice was choked with emotion as she said, "I think you're the most wonderful, dearest man I know." She kissed his cheek, but didn't give a definite answer to his proposal.

While they'd been talking, Freddie had glimpsed a dogcart with a lantern coming up the lime avenue. The cart was the only available transport for people arriving unexpectedly at Foxborough by train, there being no motor taxi cab in the village, but he hadn't paid it particular attention. Given the intense personal nature of his conversation with Amelia, he had more important things on his mind than a late-arriving guest.

When the eight-minute dinner gong rang, they joined the others in the drawing room. The butler was speaking to Lady Egeria.

"There is a person, my lady, who has come to the front door and asked for Mr. Babington." At Freddie's entrance, the butler bowed in his direction. "He gave his name as Watkins."

"Watkins?" Freddie repeated the name. "Billy? It's quite all right, Jermyn. He's an associate of mine."

"Of course your friend is welcome in our home," said Egeria. She told the butler, "Mr. Archibald Tollarhithe has left us. His room can be made ready."

"Isn't Bill Watkins your manservant?" Dotty asked Freddie.

"He is, but at the moment I'm more in need an assistant for my investigation than a valet." Freddie excused himself and followed the butler out to meet Billy.

Billy Watkins stood uncertainly just inside the front door of Foxgrove between two footmen, looking up and around the vast, oak-paneled entrance hall. His expression brightened with relief when he saw Freddie.

"Bill!" Freddie greeted him. "I'm delighted you've come, but you shouldn't have. Didn't Susan mind?"

"She saw why I had to come, and didn't say no. I couldn't sit quiet at Abbotshill once I heard about this murder," Billy replied. "I knew you'd be in the middle of it and I thought you'd need me."

"Oh, I do. We were just going in to dinner, but I'll talk to you about it tonight. Jermyn," Freddie turned to the butler, "can you please see that Billy here has some dinner and a bed?"

Jermyn had been perplexed about where to place an "associate," but he knew very well where the manservant of a guest belonged. One of the footman was told to take the suitcase, and they escorted Billy to the servants' hall.

When Freddie joined the others in the dining room, their curiosity wasn't focused on Billy's arrival nor his promotion to professional Watson, but on Freddie's announcement that he was continuing his investigation. Was that necessary now that Evelyn had been cleared? Was he working with that inspector? The Marshes recalled Deffords from his visits to Marsh Hall after the death of Bertram Marsh. When had Freddie become friends with the man? Tollarhithe opinion was divided on whether it would be horrid or thrilling to have a policeman questioning them, but Sir Percival was adamant that the police be given every assistance in following their duty.

After dinner, Phillip joined Kell and Freddie in their room to tell Billy all they'd learned since Toby's body had been discovered.

"Seems like you've done all you can with the Tollarhithes," Billy said when they'd finished. "But I couldn't've helped much with them. What about these Glovinses? Have you spoke with any of the dead lad's family or asked the other folk hereabouts that knew him?"

"Not yet," said Freddie. "Uncle Percy engaged me to look into this for the sake of the family, so we've been concentrating our efforts here and letting the police do their own work in Foxborough."

"Maybe I can get 'em to talk to me," Billy offered.

"Do you know the Glovinses, Billy?" asked Phillip, surprised.

"Never met 'em," said Billy, "but there must be things them and the other folk in Foxborough won't tell the police nor, you'll pardon me saying, one of the Tollarhithes now this lad's been killed. I'm nothing to the Tollarhithes so far as they know."

"You can't just go 'round to the butcher's shop and start asking questions," said Kell.

"I don't mean to." Billy pondered the problem of how to approach Toby's family. "There's pubs in Foxborough, aren't there?" he asked. "Would this Mr. Glovins go to one?"

"Not the father, but younger son, yes," Freddie answered. "Felix told me that he and Evelyn first met Toby and his brother in a pub."

"Which one, d'you know?"

"No, but I'll ask Felix. He'll remember."

"It's probably the Boar's Head," said Phillip. "That's the one we always go to when we're home."

Freddie confirmed this with Felix, and Billy set out by himself for Foxborough. He returned before midnight without finding Tibby, although the publican at the Boar's Head assured him that the Glovins lad was frequently there.

Late the next morning, while Deffords was interviewing the baronet's guests and family, Billy returned to the Boar's Head for a second try. After noon, a message arrived via a small boy who knocked on the front door of Foxgrove and asked for "Mr. Babington, who's staying here." When Freddie came to the door, the boy handed over the note he'd brought with him and darted off.

"It must be from Billy," Freddie said to Phillip, who'd come with him, then unfolded the square of paper. He read aloud: "'Come to B's Head, soon as you can. The Glovinses are here.'"

After making a brief search for Kell, they decided not to delay and left without him.

Kell had been sitting with his mother in one of the smaller drawing rooms, telling Deffords what they'd observed on the afternoon and evening of Toby's death. He didn't know that his two friends had gone until he went outdoors and wondered where they were.

A group of young people had gathered in the garden to remove the wilting flowers from the bower they'd constructed two days earlier. Amelia was the most keen to tear it down.

"Phil and Freddie were looking for you," Perdita informed him. "That man of Freddie's sent a note for him and off they went to the Boar's Head."

Disappointed that he'd been left behind, Kell nevertheless decided not to follow. They'd be back by tea-time and he could take this opportunity to finish another task Freddie had set him. "It must have to do with the investigation."

"Freddie, perhaps, but Phil?" Bicky laughed. "If there's a pub involved, you know he only went along for the beer."

"You can't blame him." Felix had climbed up onto the bower bench to pull down fragments of garland caught at the top of the wooden framework. "It must be hard on the lad, living in college and being away from his local brews."

"We ought to go for a sample ourselves while we're here," said Dotty. "Felix can show us the best spot."

"The Boar's Head's the best by far for local color," Felix answered as he jumped down, "but I don't suggest we go. Tibby Glovins is likely to be there. It'll only be awkward if we happen to meet him."

"Is that why Freddie went?" Mellie asked Kell. "He wanted to speak to Toby's brother?"

Kell didn't know, but given Billy's errand this morning he assumed that it was the reason.

"I hope they find out that it's someone else," said Isolde. "Some villager who had a quarrel with Toby, or a stranger. Not..." She looked at the others with solemn eyes; the words 'one of us' remained unsaid, but they were understood by all. "It's hateful to have to keep wondering about it."

"Reg is certain he's suspected," said Alma. "We don't know why, but you should hear how he goes on about Freddie's nosing in where he isn't wanted. And that policeman friend of his!"

"You can't blame the inspector for doing his

job," Amelia said curtly. She had had a long private interview with Deffords before coming out into the garden.

Kell gave her a look of sympathy. He'd been in precisely the same position only a few months ago. "Actually, you might help remove that suspicion," he told the group. "You can tell us where Reg was when Toby was killed."

"We were all here in the garden," said Alma. "We didn't see anything."

"Someone might have," Kell explained. "All us chaps were sitting... here." He paced to the spot on the lawn where the water tubs had been, stopped, and whirled to face the others; he had everyone's attention. "Our backs were to the Vixen. None of us thought to turn around and see who was behind us."

"Why would we?" asked Dotty. "We'd no idea that a murder was about to happen."

"You and I didn't look," Kell agreed, "but the girls were in the pavilion and around the bower. Felix was all over the place, running back and forth, and Piggy too. Did any of you notice Reg on the terrace?"

Several of the girls nodded eagerly. "So did I," said Felix.

"Was Phaedra with him?"

"She was," Felix confirmed, amid further yips and nods of feminine agreement. "Remember how I joked with Evvy about them being dull old folk? That's just what they looked like, she with her baby, he with his pipe, looking down at us and never coming to join the fun."

"This is too, too exciting," cried Piggy.

"But does it help Reg?" Isolde asked hopefully.

"It might," Kell answered. "Can anyone tell me when Phaedra went in, or if Reg got up before or after

Evelyn left us?"

There was uncertainty on these points. It had been growing late and the little group had been busy trying to finish their work before dark. Some of the girls noticed Phaedra leaving the terrace, but they couldn't agree on whether she'd gone in before sunset or afterwards. Perdita was sure that Reginald had been there when Evelyn had gone.

Reassured that they'd done something to help, the Tollarhithe girls cheerfully bore away the wilted flowers to the rubbish heap in a corner of the rose garden. Dotty and Bicky went with them, leaving Amelia, Felix, and Kell behind.

Amelia sighed. "It is exciting for them, as long as the Tollarhithes are safe. When it's finished, they'll go on with their lives just as before. But I can't. This murder has changed everything I'd hoped to have." A few stray, dead daisies lay scattered in the grass; she stooped to pick them up.

"That inspector chappie wasn't too beastly, was he, Mel?"

"No, not at all. It wasn't as awful as I thought it'd be. He was polite and respectful and never once said he suspected me, but all the same, I know he does. He frightens me, but he can't harm me as long as I've done nothing wrong. It isn't that. It's that once this matter is cleared up and Toby's murderer is found, I won't be married to Evvy."

"Ev does love you, Mellie," Felix told her. "He's said so often enough while I was sitting with him."

"He may say so to you, but he won't talk to me. I haven't seen him since..." She looked at the place on the lawn where she and Evelyn had been standing yesterday. "He hasn't set foot out of the Vixen since, except to attend the inquest."

"He's afraid to," Felix explained. "He's so deeply ashamed of what he's done. He can't face people, especially not you. He thinks you must hate him because of Toby."

"I don't! I only wish he'd been honest and not made such fools of both of us. Oh, maybe I am lucky to have had this escape." She turned to Kell with an odd look in her eyes. "I received an extremely kind and generous proposal from a dear friend last night. I gave him no answer then, but I've been thinking it over since."

"Have you?" Kell asked with keen interest. He'd noticed their disappearance before dinner and wondered if Freddie had said anything to her. "What did you decide?"

Amelia smiled at him. "I haven't made up my mind yet."

Felix's eyes went from one to the other during this cryptic exchange, baffled but intensely curious.

Inside the Boar's Head tavern, Phillip went to the bar to order two glasses of the local beer from the tap. He was greeted enthusiastically by some old friends on their way to the bar parlor. While Phillip chatted with them, Freddie looked around the common room and spotted Billy at the old-fashioned double settle framing the fireplace. Two other people sat with their backs toward him. As Billy waved to draw Freddie over, his companions, a boy and girl, turned to look.

Freddie let out a small gasp of surprise at the boy's familiar black mop of hair and those same soft brown, angry eyes, but this youth was a little taller than Toby and two or three years his junior. The girl was younger still, and had the same eyes.

"This is Tibby Glovins," Billy introduced the

boy, "and Miss Torie Glovins." Torie kept her eyes warily on Freddie. "The dead lad's brother and sister. This is Mr. Babington," Billy told them, "who you was asking for."

"You wanted to see me?" Freddie asked as he sat down beside Billy.

"It wasn't my idea for you to come," Billy explained apologetically, "but they heard about Sir Percival hiring a detective, and knew what I was after as soon as we started talking."

"We knew your friend here wasn't the gentleman 'tec," said Tibby, affecting the local rural accent. There was also a slight slur in his voice that suggested he'd already had a drink or two even though it wasn't long past noon. "I thought we'd better talk to you ourselves. Looking into things, are you, Mr. Babington? You'll find out who killed our Toby? Even if it's one o' the Tollarhithes?"

"Yes," said Freddie. "Even if it's a Tollarhithe. What makes you think it is?"

"Who else'd want rid of Toby?" Tibby asked back. "He was going about with their precious Mr. Evelyn and they didn't like it, so they put a stop to it."

"They did it before," said Torie. "They'd do it again."

"Before?" Freddie echoed. "When? I've never heard of another murder near Foxborough." Was she referring to the missing apprentice?

"Not a murder. Something that happened long ago," said Tibby. "Our dad told us about it before we came to live here, to warn us what the Tollarhithes was like. He said they ruled over the village like they was kings and did whatever they liked, so we'd best be careful to keep out of their way." Phillip had come to the back of the room to bring Freddie his beer;

when he overheard these words, he realized that a Tollarhithe wouldn't be welcome, silently handed Freddie a glass and went away again.

"What did they do?" Billy asked.

"As our dad tells it, there was a lad who was friends with a Tollarhithe."

"Just as Toby and Mr. Evelyn were," Torie added.

"Yes, and the high-and-mighty Tollarhithes wouldn't stand for it, so they hired somebody to beat him bloody and drive him off. He was never seen in Foxborough again."

"Surely not!" Freddie exclaimed, horrified and incredulous.

"They did, I tell you," Tibby insisted. "That's the story we heard, just as it happened."

"There's no reason for Dad to lie," his sister agreed. "What's to keep them from doing the same to Toby, only worse?"

"But if they did," said Freddie, "they wouldn't have made it look as if Evelyn were responsible."

"Who said they meant to?" Tibby retorted. "Mr. Evelyn was only going to meet Toby as he always did, and he's not arrested, is he? That's because they know he didn't kill our Toby and they know who did. You want the truth of it, Mr. Babington, you ask Sir Percival or Mr. Aubrey Tollarhithe. You'll see."

"You've never heard that story before?" Freddie asked Phillip as they returned to Foxgrove. Billy had remained in Foxborough a while longer to ask a few questions around the village at Freddie's request.

"Never," Phillip insisted. "It's almost too terrible to believe."

"But you do believe it?"

"It's only... well, I've had the feeling that there was something between that family and ours, something wrong, though I couldn't say what." Phillip tried to explain, "I was at home when Mr. Glovins first came and set up shop in Foxborough. I remember Father and Uncle Aubrey talking about it. They sounded worried. They were upset when Evelyn became friends with Toby. Not that Ev was friends with a butcher's son, but that Toby was one of the Glovinses."

Ask Sir Percival or Mr. Aubrey Tollarhithe, Tibby had said, and it seemed he was right. Was this the secret Sir Percival was afraid would come out?

9

On his return to Foxgrove, Freddie found Sir Percival in the library and repeated the story Toby's brother and sister had told him. "Is it true, Uncle Percy? Did this horrible thing happen because of the Tollarhithes years ago?"

"Oh, it's true, to the family's everlasting shame," Percival didn't look at Freddie as he answered. "And it wasn't so long ago."

"Then you do know about it?"

"How could I forget? It's the reason why neither Aubrey nor I wanted to interfere with Evelyn's friendship with Toby, much as it troubled us."

"Uncle Aubrey? Evelyn's father?" Freddie began to understand.

Percival nodded. "And Toby's father, Christopher Glovins. You've guessed that already, haven't you, Freddie?"

"I wondered if it might be so. I knew that Mr. Glovins left Foxborough abruptly when he was young and was away for many years." Freddie had asked Billy to make inquiries about any gossip or scandals involving the Glovins family, no matter how old the stories might be. "Will you tell me what actually happened? The young Glovinses know only a part of the story. I'd like to hear it all."

"I was only a boy myself at the time, not much older than Phillip," Percival began. "My father had decided I was to marry a girl from a highly respectable family who were very wealthy even if they weren't titled. The same sort of thing goes on even today—an old family wants a bit of money to keep up their estate and way of life, and a girl wants to be called Milady. I didn't kick up about it and married Miss Egeria Barclay as ordered. Things have turned out well for us, but my father and Aubrey's thought they'd make the same sort of match for him. They picked out a suitable girl, but Aubrey wouldn't agree to it. He was too attached to Christopher to give him up."

"'All the lads play, but some take it more seriously than others,'" Freddie repeated what Felix had said yesterday.

"Yes, exactly," said Percival. "Aubrey didn't say that was why he refused to marry, but of course we all knew. To make him do as they wanted, they got rid of Christopher. Uncle Archibald hired the men. After he was beaten so badly, Christopher fled, not only Foxborough, but England. He only returned after his father died and left him the butcher's shop. He hates the Tollarhithes and I can't blame him after what was done to him. I can't stop him from talking about us as he does or poisoning his children's minds against us. To try would only prove he's absolutely right in what he says. All I can do is prove him wrong by seeing that such things aren't permitted to happen while I am baronet. If a Tollarhithe has committed this crime, he mustn't be allowed to get away with it."

Sir Alvin and Aubrey's father had both died years ago. "Is it Great-Uncle Archibald?" Freddie asked. "Is that what you were afraid of when you asked me to investigate, that he's done the same again and this time it's gone too far?"

"It went too far the last time but, yes, I was afraid it was so. If it became widely known, it would be a disaster for the family. I hear that you're a bit of a radical, Freddie. You know better than I what those Bolshies are saying about our class. If it were widely known that Tollarhithes, including the last baronet, my father, hired ruffians to beat a Foxborough boy, it would be the perfect sort of thing to use against us. If it's happened again..." He shook his head in dismay. "I hoped that if you learned the truth of the matter before the police did, I might be able to tend to it privately. It does look as if my worst fears are true. It's been done again and I can't think who else could be responsible."

"Aubrey?" Freddie guessed.

"No!" Percival rejected the idea. "Not Aubrey. I know him better than anyone. I see how this tragedy's brought that other incident back to him. He feels it almost as if Toby were Christopher all over again. He'd never hurt his son in the same way he'd been hurt." Then he added, "Any more than I would hurt Phil. The only son I have now. He never comes home and when he does, he avoids me."

It occurred to Freddie that he'd spent more time during this visit in Sir Percival's company than Phillip had. "That's because he's afraid," he told Percival. "He thinks you must be furious with him over...well, Kell."

"I'm not angry with him. Oh, I was, at first,"

Percival admitted. "Then I remembered how it was with Aubrey and I won't see that repeated. Some men would say they'd rather their son be dead than homosexual. But I have one dead son and I say I'd rather have the other one alive even if he were the worst sort of degenerate."

"Phillip isn't degenerate," Freddie protested. "He's a thoroughly nice boy. He's loyal, honest, brave, all the things Lord Baden-Powell would have the youth of Britain be."

Percival smiled. "The less said about his obedience and thrift, the better, but I take your point. There's nothing much wrong with the boy besides taking his hero-worship for Kell too far. It's something most lads go through at school, then grow out of when they meet the right girl. Phil's not yet twenty-one. There's plenty of time."

When he left Percival, Freddie went next door to the Vixen. The garden door to the study was open; he ventured inside to find Aubrey in his comfortable chair by the hearth, busy working on a half-finished figure which appeared to be a leaping deer. Freddie recalled that Isolde had said her father carved woodwork when he had something on his mind, and that Aubrey had been brooding lately. "Uncle Aubrey?"

Aubrey looked up, realizing that he had a visitor, and set his work aside. "Ah, Freddie. Come to ask questions for yourself this time, instead of sending Phil?" He tried to sound as if he were joking, but he was wary, Freddie could see it.

"I thought I'd better. It's rather personal." He stepped into the room and shut the door. "I've come to ask about your boyhood friendship with Christopher Glovins, and how it ended."

Aubrey stared at him, then shut his eyes. "So that's come out at last." He sounded dismayed, but resigned. "I knew it must eventually, but I've been dreading it. Did Phillip put you on to it? He told you what I said about Archibald?"

Was that what Phillip was keeping from them? "No, it wasn't Phil," Freddie replied. "Toby's brother and sister told me part of the story, with no names. When I asked Uncle Percy, he told me the rest. He's afraid that the same thing has happened again with Toby."

"So am I, Freddie. So am I." Aubrey lifted his eyes to the young man. "Have you spoken to anyone else about this? Do my children know?"

"No," Freddie reassured him. "I'm certain they don't."

"I'm glad of that, at least. It'd be too great a shock to them. I wanted to talk to Evelyn before his wedding, to be certain that he was marrying Mellie for the right reasons. Poor Evvy. He's weeping, heartbroken, and I don't know if it's for Mellie's sake or Toby's. I didn't want him to feel pushed into this marriage, as I'd been, but I delayed too long." Aubrey's gaze dropped. "I was afraid to say that I was speaking from my own experience. It's a hard thing to tell your child that the marriage that made him was an unhappy one. I never blamed Eva. It wasn't her fault. No one can say I didn't do my proper duty as a husband, but I never loved her as I ought to and she felt that. It's a terrible thing, Freddie, to fall in love with the wrong person, the wrong sex, the wrong class, everything wrong, and there's nothing you can do. It's the worst thing in the world. You can't possibly know."

He sounded so utterly ashamed that Freddie's heart went out to him. On an impulse, he said, "Uncle

Aubrey, believe me, please. I am sympathetic."

Aubrey lifted his head and met Freddie's eyes. "Are you?"

"You know that Kell Marsh is my dearest friend, like a brother to me." He imagined that Sir Percival must have a similar bond with his own cousin and had the same protective feelings toward him, although Kell wasn't as fragile as Aubrey. "I won't tell anyone, except for Phillip and Kell. I think Phil would be heartened to know. He's so fond of you."

"And still will be?" Aubrey gave him a small, wry smile. "I'm fond of him too. Phil's a good lad, full of mischief, but there's no harm in him. Things are different these days. We didn't even dare whisper our secrets when I was young, nor imagine speaking of them aloud. Phillip and Kell have a courageousness that I never did. If I had, I might've gone after Christopher when I learned what had happened to him. I should have, but I was too afraid of what might happen to me if I didn't behave. I agreed to do whatever my father wanted."

"May I ask?" said Freddie. "Do you know who beat Mr. Glovins when he was a boy?"

"We could never find out. Archibald protected them. He was the one who arranged it all. Even after my father and Pal's father were gone, he wouldn't tell us whom he'd hired. You can be sure if I'd known their names or where I could find them, I would have..." Aubrey stopped and shook his head. "I like to believe I'd have repaid them for what they did to Christopher. At least, I would've told Pal so that he could see them punished."

"I should've guessed," Phillip said when Freddie told him. "I see now why Father hasn't been pushing me as hard as he might. Poor Uncle Aubrey! He's been so kind since he heard about Kell and me. Now I understand why."

"But you see what this means, don't you?" said Freddie. "We've wasted time trying to find out where everyone was when Toby was killed, and it doesn't matter. It makes no difference if Mellie's left-handed or Reg hasn't got a left hand at all. If the person who actually stabbed Toby was hired to do it, then the person who hired him could've been sitting comfortably at home or constantly in sight of a dozen people." The idea actually brought him a sense of relief; while Mellie might just conceivably strike out at her rival in a moment of jealousy or anger, she was hardly likely to have hired ruffians to murder him.

"So what do we do next?" Kell asked.

"We need to find out who was hired."

"But how? Who could they possibly have hired? I can't imagine any of the local folk saying, 'as you wish' if even Uncle Percy himself asked them to commit murder. The most feudally-minded would balk at that."

"Could it be the same ones that were hired the first time?" Phillip wondered.

"That was over thirty years ago," said Kell.

"They might still be about," Freddie said. "They'd commit a crime of violence for a Tollarhithe. They've done so once before. Uncles Percival and Aubrey don't know who they are, but at least one person certainly does. Perhaps two."

"You mean Great-Uncle Archibald?" asked Phillip.

Freddie nodded. "We haven't given him much of our attention, but it's time we did."

"You heard the things he said to me, Freddie,"

Kell said. "He'd 'put a stop' to the likes of me. What if he did 'put a stop' to Toby?"

"By the way, Phil, what did Uncle Aubrey say about Archibald?" Freddie asked him. "That secret's out now. Will you tell us?"

The question caught Phillip off guard. His face flushed and he looked embarrassed and very contrite as he answered, "Only that Archibald must've had a hand in it. He wouldn't say why he thought so. He made me promise not to tell to you about it."

"And you agreed to that?" Kell asked, ruffled at this mild betrayal.

"He's my favorite uncle!" Phillip replied in his own defense. "What else could I do? I said I wouldn't tell if there wasn't anything in it."

"Well, it turns out there is," Kell retorted.

"I suppose he was afraid that if we looked into it, we'd find out about him and Toby's father," Freddie said.

"He kept it secret for so long." Phillip's sympathies remained firmly with Aubrey. "At least, it wasn't me that told."

When Billy returned from Foxborough, Freddie asked him, "What did you find out?"

"I asked 'round like you said to," Billy began his report. "But it's an odd thing, that story Miss Glovins and her brother told us isn't known hereabouts, not even by the old folk. You'd think, horrible as it was, if it'd happened in the last hundred years somebody'd remember hearing about it."

"What do they say about Mr. Glovins?" asked Freddie. "Do they recall when he left?"

Billy nodded. "Some folks say Christopher Glovins ran off as a lad without a word. It upset his father something terrible. Nobody knew where he'd gone 'til he came home again years afterwards with his children."

"He never told anyone why he left? He doesn't tell that story?"

"Not that I've found out," Billy answered; he hadn't connected the two himself. "He's not popular with his neighbors. They say he speaks ill of the Tollarhithes every chance he gets. It's cost him some business from them who don't like that sort of talk, but he never says just what the Tollarhithes did to him."

"So he's kept it secret too," Freddie mused.

"Too?" said Billy. "Now what've I been missing?"

While Kell and Phillip explained to Billy what he'd missed, Freddie went on softly, thinking aloud more than speaking to his friends: "He told his children, but not enough for them to realize that he was referring to himself. Even after all these years, Mr. Glovins must be ashamed to have it known what was once between him and Uncle Aubrey."

"You're going to see this old Mr. Archibald?" Billy asked Freddie, breaking into his thoughts.

"What? Oh, yes. I'd thought I'd call at his cottage tomorrow to ask him whom he hired and if they're still around."

"Begging your pardon, but wouldn't Mr. Glovins know too? He must've seen who it was that beat him. It'll be a shorter trip to find out the same thing. I won't have you running over to this old gent's house when your answer might be right here in the village."

Freddie smiled. He'd missed Billy's fussing over his health. "We'll go to Foxborough first," he agreed, "before we seek out Uncle Archibald." He meant to speak to Christopher Glovins in any case.

"If you don't mind," said Kell. "Phil and I won't come along."

"I know how Mr. Glovins feels about Tollarhithes," Phillip added.

"Besides," Kell grinned, "if you do go to see old Archibald, he'll be more amenable to talk to you if we 'fancy-lads' aren't there."

10

The next morning, Freddie went into Foxborough, accompanied by Billy. They encountered Inspector Deffords in front of the Grapes; the inspector had heard about a mysterious stranger asking questions around the village, but guessed it must be one of Freddie's friends. Like Kell, Billy hadn't forgotten the events of the previous spring, when they'd been desperate to keep certain information from Deffords, and he regarded the inspector warily.

Freddie himself had avoided Deffords the day before. After their conversation about Amelia being a suspect, he didn't want the inspector to know that his response had been a marriage proposal. He didn't want Billy to know about it either, not until he knew how Amelia was going to answer.

"A young man was found by the side of the road near Bog Wood the night before last, after being struck by a lorry," Deffords told them. "That's barely three miles away. He was taken to the nearest hospital, badly injured and not expected to live. He hasn't been identified, but the local constable thinks it might be our missing butcher-boy. If you learn anything important, you can telephone me at the Wymondham

Constabulary. I'll get your message even if I'm not in. How's your work for Sir Percival getting on?"

"We're going to see Mr. Glovins today, if he'll see us," Freddie replied evasively. "Did you manage to interview all the Tollarhithes?"

"Most of them, though they didn't tell me anything I didn't already know. Only Sir Percival and that fair-haired boy, Felix, admit they knew about the friendship between Toby Glovins and Evelyn Tollarhithe. Her ladyship denies she even knew Toby existed."

"What about Amelia?" asked Freddie. "Have you cleared up matters with her?"

"Miss Marsh says she didn't leave her room, but can't produce anyone who saw her during the hour before she came down to join you in the garden. We had a long talk about Toby Glovins and how well she knew him." Deffords added sympathetically, "You'll be relieved to hear that she signed her statement with her right hand."

The butcher's shop, just off the high street, had been closed for business the day before. Its door was open today and wares in the form of ropes of linked sausages and plucked fowl were on display. After Deffords had gone, Freddie and Billy went inside. Torie Glovins was at the shop counter. She informed them that she could sell what was at hand and would take larger orders. "Anybody that wants a fancy cut o' beef or chops'll have to wait 'til Dad feels up to his work."

"How's your dad?" Billy inquired respectfully.

Torie shook her head. "Since the police brought us news of Toby, he sits in the back parlor," she indicated a curtained doorway at the back of the shop. "We had to lay Toby out there 'til he's buried.

Dad's done naught but weep over him. It's hit him terrible hard." Tears filled her soft brown eyes. She didn't look angry now, only very young and worried for her father. "It's not only Toby, but Benny's missing too. He keeps asking if they found him yet."

Freddie decided not to tell her about the youth who'd been run over. Deffords had told him in confidence, and there was no reason to upset the Glovins family before the police confirmed that it was the missing apprentice.

"Is he that fond of the lad?" asked Billy.

"He's looked after Benny since we first came here," said Torie. "Benny worked for our granddad and when Dad took the shop, he kept him on. He took pity on him. Benny's a big, thick-headed lad, you see, good at chopping meats and carrying heavy sides about, but he could never run a shop on his own."

"Was he here the night Toby was killed?" Freddie asked.

The girl nodded. "He shut up shop at six, same as always. I heard Dad say goodnight, and that's the last we saw of Benny. He lives with his mother, but he never went home that night. He's all she's got in the world." She considered Freddie. "Did you come to talk to Dad, Mr. Babington? I'll ask if he'll see you, but he mayn't be fit for company."

"I'd be grateful if you would," Freddie replied. "I'd like to ask you a few questions too, Miss Glovins. That story you told me, did you or your brother tell it to the police as well?"

"Tibby wanted to, but Dad stopped him. He said it wouldn't be believed, and anyway, the police was in Sir Percival's pocket."

"But you told me, even though I'm working for Sir Percival."

"You said you were going to see justice done, even if it was against the Tollarhithes," Torie explained. "We wanted to see if you meant it." Billy looked indignant that she doubted Freddie's word. Freddie laid a hand on his arm to keep him silent. "Did you repeat it to Sir Percival?" the girl asked. "What did he say about it?"

"He told me it was true, and he told me more. Torie, did you know who the boy in your story was when you told it to me? Did you know it was your father?"

Torie focused her attention on wiping the butcher's block, even though it was perfectly clean. "Dad never said so, but we guessed," she admitted. "Before we came to live here, he told us about the Tollarhithes. We saw how he hated them. When Toby became friends with Mr. Evelyn, Dad had a talk with him. I couldn't hear all they said, but I could see he wasn't pleased. He showed Toby a knife he said belonged to a Tollarhithe."

"A knife?" Billy eyed the set of long, sharp blades and shining cleavers arrayed behind the butcher's block.

Torie followed his gaze. "Oh, not one of those! A little thing. Dad said it was a gift, a pledge of a friendship that'd gone wrong."

From the parlor behind the curtained doorway, a hoarse and thick-sounding voice called out, "Torie, who's that you're talking to? Is it a customer?"

"No, Dad!" Torie shouted back. "They've come about Toby."

Mr. Glovins came out. He was a brawnier man than his sons and didn't have what Freddie had come to think of as the Glovins eyes. In this respect, all three children must take after their late French-

Canadian mother.

Mr. Glovins studied him in return. "Who're you lads? I don't know you." He glanced at Billy. "You're not the police. They've been here already."

"It's Mr. Babington, Dad," Torie explained. "You remember, we told you? Sir Percival's investigator."

"Sir Percival's investigator?" Christopher Glovins echoed incredulously. "You can't be much older'n my own boys."

"Not much older," Freddie agreed, "but I have some experience in these matters. I'm very sorry about your son, Mr. Glovins. I mean to do all I can for him."

A shudder rippled through the older man and, to Freddie's astonishment, he laughed. "Thank you, lad, but my Toby's beyond all help."

His daughter rushed to his side, but Glovins waved her away. After a moment, he pulled himself together. "So, you're working for Percy Tollarhithe?" he asked. "I knew him as a boy, though I haven't seen much of him since. Has he grown into the sort of man his father was?"

"No, Mr. Glovins." Freddie had barely known Sir Alvin, but he'd formed no good opinion of the last baronet. After spending so much time with Sir Percival, Freddie had also developed a new respect for Phillip's father; Percival might be concerned with how things looked, but he would also do what was right. "You're mistaken if you imagine he's like his father. He's a fair-minded and honest man, even if he is a baronet." With Mr. Glovins, Freddie thought he could be blunt. "He's very much ashamed of the crime that was committed against you by the Tollarhithes."

Mr. Glovins looked bewildered and turned to his daughter.

"We told him, Dad," Torie confessed.

"It's why we're here, Mr. Glovins," Freddie explained. "I thought you might be able to tell me who it was who beat you."

"Why d'you want to know about that? It was over and done so long ago. What's it got to do with Toby?"

"Sir Percival thinks it might be the same men."

Mr. Glovins laughed again, with a frightening, wild note. "I don't know! I never did. There was two of them, laborers, probably from one of the farms. It was nobody I knew. I didn't recognize their voices. I never saw their faces. It was dark. I was walking home after seeing... my friend. I can't tell you more." He retreated back through the curtain. With a despairing glance at the two visitors, Torie went after him.

As they left the shop, Freddie said, "I'm sorry, Billy. We'll have to see Uncle Archibald after all."

Freddie borrowed Kell's roadster and had Billy drive. They stopped to ask for directions twice once they were in the vicinity of Aylsham, but eventually located Archibald's cottage on a narrow, winding lane far from any neighbors.

At the sound of the motor, Archibald came to the cottage door to peer out. "Why it's young Freddie Marsh... no, it's Babington, isn't it?" the old man said as Freddie approached the garden gate. He regarded Billy, whom he'd never seen before, with curiosity, but Billy remained with the roadster while Freddie entered the garden. "What brings you here?"

"I'd like to talk to you," Freddie requested. "May I come in?"

Archibald still looked curious, but he nodded.

Billy watched anxiously as Freddie accompanied

the elderly man inside, but Freddie himself was unafraid. In spite of all he knew about Archibald and all he suspected, he didn't believe he was in any danger.

The small front parlor was a mess. The old man's shirt and worn velveteen jacket were stained with tobacco juice. A half-dozen empty and dirty cups and mugs sat around the room, and the browned peelings and core of an apple sat next to a small knife on a plate.

"I don't have many visitors," Archibald said as he offered his guest a seat.

"You must be lonely, living out here," Freddie began. "I understand that you quarreled with Uncle Percy ages ago and moved away rather than make it up."

"I made my choice, and I've grown accustomed to it," Archibald answered with grim good humor. "I prefer this peace and quiet over the gabbling of so many fools in Foxborough. It's not as it was in Sir Alvin's day. Percy's father knew how to keep order in his house, and in his family. Percy's too lax in that regard. Lets his children run wild. Well, I'm invited now and again, to see the young ones wed. It pleases me to see a wedding, although this last one didn't come off as planned. I hear it won't come off at all now."

"Yes, that's so," said Freddie. "Evelyn's broken off with Amelia."

"Young Evelyn's a blasted fool. What decent young man wouldn't want to marry a sweet, pretty girl like that Marsh cousin of yours? If his father and Percival knew what was going on, they should've put the boy right before it led to this trouble."

"Actually," Freddie ventured, "that's what I've come to talk to you about. Toby Glovins's death. I don't know if you've heard, Uncle Percival's asked me to look into it."

"I don't know what I can tell you," said Archibald. "I don't know a thing about it. Why come to me?"

"Because," Freddie advanced boldly now, "I've been told that something similar happened once, over thirty years ago, to another Glovins boy. Toby's father, in fact."

Archibald drew back as if Freddie had physically flung something at him. "'Been told'!" he repeated. "'Been told.' And I can guess by whom! Percy or Aubrey, or both of them? They've held it against me all these years. I suppose they're trying to lay this murder at my doorstep in revenge."

"You don't think they've reason to bear a grudge?" Freddie asked, trying to keep the acid note from his voice.

"Not at all. What I did was for the good of the Tollarhithes. It's a young man's duty to marry as his family thinks best, and Aubrey refused. His father and Sir Alvin despaired. When they asked for my help, I was glad to be of service. It all came out right in the end. What does Aubrey have to complain of? He had a beautiful wife who gave him four children. Christopher Glovins has children too that wouldn't have been born if he hadn't run away. Ask them if they regret their sons and daughters. Ask Phaedra if she'd rather not have that new baby of hers, fathered by Aubrey's Reginald? How many children would never have existed if it weren't for my intervention?"

Freddie grew sickened as he listened to this and realized that the old man wasn't in the least ashamed of the appalling thing he'd done. He sounded proud. "There's one less now."

"Do you believe I had something to do with that?" The old man laughed. "If you've come to accuse me, you've come to the wrong place. I tell you," He leaned forward and tapped on Freddie's chest with a forefinger. Freddie flinched at the touch. "I never knew of it until after the boy was dead. It was no business of mine to intervene, even if I had. If anyone should've acted to ensure that Evelyn married, it was his father—but of course Aubrey wouldn't do the proper thing."

"Wh– What did you do?" Freddie asked. "That other time, when Sir Alvin asked for your help?"

"Why do you want to know?"

"I want to know who you hired to beat Christopher Glovins."

"Why should I tell you?" Archibald shot back. "I would never tell Percival, and you'll go straight to him. Do you think I don't know what he'd do to them if he knew where to find them?"

Freddie had been reluctant to use the authority Sir Percival had given him to force Archibald to cooperate. Who knew how far the old man could be pushed? What if it he merely laughed and refused to speak? Archibald had, after all, chosen to leave Foxborough and live in virtual exile rather than surrender that information.

"You'll tell me," said Freddie, trying another tactic, "because this time it's murder. You put a stop to a friendship between a Tollarhithe and a Glovins once. It's happened again, only now the Glovins boy has been stabbed to death, not merely beaten and driven away. What do you think Uncle Percival will do about that?"

"I had nothing to do with it!" Archibald insisted.

"You did before. Who will believe otherwise now? Even if I take you at your word, you know he won't. You said yourself that Sir Percival has it in for you. What if it's the same men that you hired? That only makes it worse for you, whether you're involved this time or not." Freddie focused his disgust and anger at this old man. He wanted Archibald to be frightened, and he was gratified to see that his words had some effect. Archibald had grown pale. "It's noble of you to want to protect your friends, but will you protect murderers? Will you hang in their place? Now, tell me: Who did you hire?"

"It can't be the same men, not after so long. I haven't seen them to speak to in over twenty years. They were a pair of farmhands. Brothers."

"Their names?" Freddie pressed.

"Twigg. Jabez and Enoch Twigg."

"Do they still live near Foxborough?"

"Why shouldn't they? As a matter of fact, they have their own farm now, a freehold granted by Sir Alvin." Archibald had been intimidated, but he hadn't lost his spirit. "They were well rewarded for their services to our family."

Billy stood waiting outside the cottage door. He'd drawn closer at the sound of raised voices, ready to be of help if Freddie needed him. When Freddie came out, he looked shocked at what he'd overheard.

Freddie was white-faced and trembling as he passed through the garden and out of the gate. "Let's get away from here," he said.

"I never saw you in such a state!" Billy said a short while later. Freddie had driven them away from the cottage, but was too shaken to go far. A couple of miles down the lane, he pulled over beside an old well. While Billy refilled the radiator, Freddie sat on the grass and tried to calm down. "I never saw you be cruel before."

"I've never felt so angry before," said Freddie. "That infuriating, evil-minded old man has caused so much unhappiness, and he's proud of it! I wanted to frighten him. I wanted to punish him. I try to understand the reasons why people do evil things. We've seen worse among the Germans and even the English, but this was much more personal, Billy. It's people like him that make it so difficult for Kell and Phil to live their lives in peace and privacy. I lost my temper."

"I can't say as I blame you," Billy admitted. "What about this Mr. Archibald? D'you think he did it?"

"No. Awful as he is, I believe he told the truth when he said he didn't know about Toby and Evelyn. He didn't hire any ruffians, this time." Archibald had done his best to protect the people he'd hired all those years ago, but what if someone else had found out who they were? Freddie got up. "We ought to go and see the Twiggs."

"What, now? I thought we'd go back to Foxgrove. You shouldn't push yourself so hard, Freddie. You're working yourself up into a bad turn."

"If we go back now, we'll only have to drive around again tomorrow," Freddie answered. "Uncle Archibald said the Twiggs had a farm not far from Foxborough, but he didn't say exactly where. The neighbors will know." He climbed into the passenger seat of the roadster. "We'd best get on with it if we want to return to Foxgrove by tea-time. I promise I'll rest before dinner."

The Twigg farm wasn't difficult to locate. Billy and Freddie stopped at the next village they came to and the local publican gave them directions as well as a warning that the Twiggs kept to themselves.

The farm appeared to be small but prosperous: recently harvested fields of hay, a dozen cows in the pasture, hogs in a penned yard, and chickens, geese, and ducks wandering. A stone wall bounded the property and a wide wooden gate opened onto a private cart track that led to a barn and other outbuildings.

Billy would have preferred to go in and speak to the Twiggs in Freddie's place, but Freddie insisted, "No, Bill. I think that in this case, a relative of the Tollarhithes will be of greater use."

He left Billy in the lane with the roadster. As he opened the gate, he was greeted by a barking dog. A sturdy young man came out of the barn. When Freddie explained why he was there, the youth replied that "Dad and Uncle Enoch were up t' house," and held the dog by its collar until Freddie had gone past.

Freddie went up the cart track, past the outbuildings, until he came to the farmhouse. Two elderly men sat in the dooryard, smoking their pipes and enjoying the sunny afternoon. One was whittling a stick of wood. They looked as gnarled and tough as old tree roots. Freddie could see that they had once been large and strong like the son he'd met at the gate, used to long hours of hard work, but they were long past their prime. If they'd been mature men when Archibald had hired them, they must be well into their sixties or even seventies.

The brothers seemed curious but not wary at the sight of their visitor. The one who was whittling nodded and said, "Aft'n to ye, young sir. We don't see much of quality folk in these parts. Lost, are ye?"

"As a matter of fact," said Freddie, "I'm staying at Foxgrove."

"Ah!" The old man smiled. "Visiting the Tollarhithes? Are ye one o' the family?"

"Yes, sort of." Freddie didn't know if he was addressing Jabez or Enoch. "My great-grandmother was a Tollarhithe, Miranda Tollarhithe. She was Sir Percival's great-aunt. Frederick Babington is my name."

The mention of his ancestress was enough for Freddie to gain the Twiggs' acceptance. Miss Miranda was before their time, but they agreed that a great-grandson of a Tollarhithe lady was welcome on their farm.

"Are you Mr. Twigg?" Freddie asked the one who had spoken to him.

"Enoch Twigg," the old man replied. "This here is Jabez, my brother. What can we do for you, Mr. Babington?"

"If you don't mind, I'd like to ask you a few questions about something that happened a long time ago." He broached the subject carefully, for he thought that the Twiggs would mind very much if he went at this the wrong way. "Do you know a man named Christopher Glovins?"

"Glovins?" The brothers consulted their memories. "There was once Glovinses hereabouts."

"He's the Foxborough butcher," Freddie prompted.

"Oh, him! Butcher Glovins died a while ago," said Jabez. "We don't have no need of a butcher's services. We kill and dress our own meat for the table."

Freddie began to wonder if Jabez hadn't grown feeble-minded with his advanced years. "Christopher Glovins took over his father's business when the old butcher died," he explained. "I believe you knew him when he was a boy." He ventured further, "I've heard a story that Sir Alvin and some of the other Tollarhithe gentlemen... ah, paid you to see that he left Foxborough."

Enoch was suddenly on his guard. "Who's been carrying such tales against us?"

"Then it's not true?" asked Freddie.

"Not as such. Why d'ye want to go digging up summat from years ago as no one remembers?"

"I remember it. Buggers, they was!" Jabez spat so vituperatively that Freddie jumped, startled, and felt the blood rush to his face. "Filthy buggers. 'Tisn't natural, and we did right to put a stop to it."

"Beg yer pardon!" Enoch exclaimed, observing their visitor's shocked expression. "You mustn't mind Jabez. He means no harm. You mind your language with the young gent, Jabez!"

"What about this business with Christopher Glovins?" Freddie persisted. "It did happen, didn't it, just as your brother says?"

"Ah," Enoch conceded, "I didn't mean to lie t'ye, young sir. We was told to keep our mouths shut about it and keep 'em shut we have—'til today." He scowled at his brother. "You won't go carrying it no further, will ye? Sir Percival'd take against us if he heard." He was obviously afraid that Freddie would tell. "What we did was in aid of the old master. One o' the common-folk was getting above himself and wanting to be put back in his proper place. 'Twas for the best. Didn't the troublesome Tollarhithe lad see sense after that and marry as his family wanted?"

Freddie wanted desperately to get away. Sick and angry after his conversation with Archibald, he didn't want to face more of this ugliness. The worst of it was that he knew that these two were only saying in blunt and vulgar terms exactly what the late Sir Alvin,

Aubrey's father, and Archibald had believed. But he had come here for a reason and couldn't leave until his questions had been answered. "What I wanted to know, Mr. Twigg, is if anyone else has come to ask you about it lately—you, or any of your family?" Freddie glanced over his shoulder toward the barn, thinking of that strapping young man who'd let him in.

"None," said Enoch.

"No one's asked you if one of your family might do another service for the Tollarhithes?"

"No! Now, grandson of a Tollarhithe or no, Mr. Babington, that's enough prying. I'll have to ask you to be off."

Freddie had worn out his welcome, but he was glad to leave.

11

"'Filthy buggers'!" Kell laughed. "Did they really say that?" He sat at the foot of Phillip's bed, rocking with amusement at Freddie's report of his conversation with the Twigg brothers.

"One of them did," said Freddie. "It wasn't funny, Kell. It was awful. They were as repulsive a pair of louts as I've ever met, except for the gentlemen who put them up to it." He added this last part hesitantly, knowing that one of the gentlemen had been Phillip's and Kell's grandfather. To his relief, they didn't take offense.

"I was only eight years old when Grandfather died," said Phillip. "We were barely acquainted. It's not as if it were Father."

"Poor Freddie," Kell said with more sympathy. "It must've been beastly for you standing there and listening to that bile spewing from a dotty old farmer.

But old as these Twigg fellows are, they couldn't have done it this time, could they?"

"I can't see it. Jabez seems quite senile, and Enoch's too afraid of being found out by Uncle Percy. Besides, even if they were willing to repeat their service to the Tollarhithes, neither of them would be a match for a fit young man like Toby Glovins."

"One of 'em had that son who let you in," said Billy. "What about him?"

"It's possible. There might be other young lads around the farm I didn't see. Someone might've approached and hired one of them." But Freddie realized that this was a faint prospect. They'd followed their clues to a blind end; the investigation could go no further along these lines.

"Are you going to tell Father, Freddie?" asked Phillip. "About the Twiggs, I mean."

Freddie shook his head. The thought of seeing those two horrible old men get what was coming to them had its appeal, but there were other factors to consider. He'd have to speak with Percival in any case.

As he'd promised, Freddie went to his room to lie down, but when Billy looked in on him half an hour later, he found Freddie lying with his eyes open. "Can't you sleep?"

"I'm afraid not." Freddie sighed. "I've too much to think about."

Billy didn't ask what Freddie was thinking of; he knew very well. "Investigating's always hard on you when you start suspecting your own relatives."

"In that respect, it's worse for Phil this time. It's his family after all. I think he's particularly worried for Uncle Aubrey, though I don't know why. The way Aubrey and Uncle Percy feel about what happened to Christopher Glovins, I can't believe they'd ever let such a horrible thing be repeated while they had it in their power to prevent it." He sat up. "That's the worst part of it, Bill, even worse than suspecting one's relatives of murder. Whenever I begin looking into things, I discover ugly secrets about people I'd rather not know."

"What happened with Mr. Archibald 'n' these Twiggs?"

"Yes, and Sir Alvin as well. I used to look on jolly old England as a green and pleasant land, especially when we were away from it. I saw there were injustices and inequalities and a great deal that needed to be improved, but I believed we were at heart a nation of decent people. Yet that ugliness has always been festering underneath."

"I suppose it has," Billy answered slowly, "but it hasn't poisoned everything. There's lots of decent folk too."

Freddie gave his friend an affectionate smile. "Indeed there are. What about you and Susan Baines? Did you propose to her while you were in Abbotshill?" Billy hadn't mentioned his sweetheart since he'd first arrived.

"We haven't settled matters yet, only talked about how it'd be if we got married. Sorting out the business, you might say. I told her how you're going to make over part of the London flat for us. That's all."

"Is that all, Billy?" Freddie recalled what Amelia had said about getting on ahead of the wedding night. "You and she, you haven't...?"

"No!" Billy blushed, shocked at the delicate question. "What d'you think? Sue's a nice girl!"

"I don't doubt it. All the same, nice girls and boys sometimes do."

"Well, we haven't— and we won't!" Billy insisted. "Not 'til we're proper married." He regarded Freddie with some confusion. "Why d'you ask? You haven't changed your mind about me marrying, have you? I thought you were keen for it. You pushed me off to see Sue quick enough."

"No, Billy, I wouldn't do that. You and Susan have my blessings. I want you both to be happy. It's only that I've been thinking about making some greater changes to our household."

Billy didn't understand. "You mean, that old box room we don't use? You said it'd make a nice nursery."

"We might need more room than that. I thought that when we return to London, we might look for a larger flat, one where you and Susan could bring up children without crowding, and I would have all the room I needed."

"Room for what?"

"Guests. Kell seems determined to make himself at home, and you know Phillip likes to come up whenever he can. And there's Amelia," Freddie said, broaching the idea gently; he knew that Billy wouldn't be as pleased about his own prospective marriage as he was about Billy's. "This trouble with Evelyn has been terribly distressing for her. Since he threw her over, I thought she might like to get away. I've... ah, invited her to come and stay for as long as she likes."

"Did you?" Billy seemed nonplussed at this news. "Is she coming?"

"She hasn't said so yet. You don't mind, do you?"

"No," Billy responded. "You've a right to have whoever you like in your own home."

"Thank you, Billy." Freddie could bring the

subject further along if necessary, but he'd said enough for now. "I knew you wouldn't let me down."

The conversation over dinner that night wasn't about the murder, nor directly concerned with Amelia's and Evelyn's situation. Diana observed that other guests who had come to Foxborough for the cancelled wedding had left, but she intended to stay and assist Egeria until "that other problem" was resolved. The ladies from Marsh Hall were also making plans to go.

"We'll leave the day after tomorrow," Emily decided. "Mellie dear, will you be coming with us?"

"I can't tell yet," Amelia answered. "There are some matters I haven't settled." She glanced in Freddie's direction.

Freddie hadn't had a chance to speak privately with Amelia since the previous night, but he'd caught her watching him in odd moments. As they left the dining room, he had only to say, "Mellie?" softly for her to stop and turn. "A word, please?"

"Kell told me what you said to him yesterday, about considering my offer," Freddie said once they were alone. "Is that what you haven't settled yet?"

"Yes, in part. It was very gallant of you to ask, and there are reasons I might accept. I can't stay here and I can't help thinking how humiliating it'd be to go home again unmarried. It'd please Mother and the rest of the family if we married, especially after all this. I'd enjoy living in London. And I'd be able to wear my white dress after all. If it weren't for Evelyn, there's no one else I'd rather marry. I realize that sounds frivolous." She folded her hands in her lap and announced, "On the other hand, there *is* Evvy, you see."

"I know you're still in love with him, if that's what you mean."

"Yes. Idiotic of me under the circumstances, but I can't help it. You can't change the feelings of a lifetime overnight, even when you'd like to. I do care for you very dearly, Freddie, but I don't love you in that way. If I don't rush to accept your proposal, that's why. Can you possibly want to marry me, knowing how I feel?"

"I do understand that you'll need a little time to make an adjustment," Freddie reassured her. "There's no hurry. Go back to Marsh Hall to think things over, or come and visit me in London before you make up your mind. Keep my offer in reserve, if you like." He asked, "Are you going to try to win Evelyn back? Do you want to, after he's been such a brute?"

"After all that's happened, I should be glad never to see him again. It'd be different if Toby were still alive, but Toby's gone. I must at least see Evvy and speak to him before I give him up for good."

When Freddie left Amelia, he sought Sir Percival in the library. "I only wanted to tell you that it's not as you feared," Freddie informed him. "It can't be the same men who took part in that other crime years ago. I'm convinced they aren't involved in Toby's death."

Percival looked surprised. "Is that where you were today? You've seen them?"

"I spoke to Great-Uncle Archibald, and..." Freddie paused before he went on, "two old farmers."

"So, you've found out who they are, but you don't want to tell me?"

"I will if you ask and you may deal with them as you see fit... only, I think it might do more harm than good to see them receive their just deserts at this late date." The Twiggs deserved everything that Sir Percival could to do to punish them, including losing the farm they'd received as a reward for their brutal service, but in the long years since, they'd grown into a state where they could scarcely be expected to fend for themselves if they were cast from their home. And what of the younger Twiggs who had no part in their elders' crime? They might not even be aware of it. Was it fair that they should suffer?

"You ask for mercy for them?"

"Not so much for their sakes, Uncle. There are other people to consider, yourself included. As you say, I've seen them. I've spoken with them. They're quite old now and enfeebled. One has gone dotty. They aren't repentant, but they are very much afraid of what will happen to them if you should ever find them out. At least, the one who's still in his right senses is. I'm sure that whatever you do with them would be just, but in this case, justice would look like cruelty."

"I see." As Freddie had anticipated, Percival appreciated how very bad it would appear if he were to punish two elderly men for a decades-old crime. To explain his reasons would expose his father and his family to greater shame. "Perhaps it's best if I don't know their names. As much as I'd like to see them receive their just deserts, I don't believe I could rely on my restraint."

"Do you want me to go on looking into this?" Freddie asked. "I haven't found Toby's murderer." While he didn't like the idea of leaving that crime unsolved, he'd done all he'd been asked to do: Evelyn was under no suspicion and Sir Percival's fears had been traced to their source and determined to be unfounded.

Percival gave the question some thought. "No," he decided at last. "It doesn't appear we're responsible for that boy's death. Leave the rest of it to the police.

You can tell your inspector friend whatever you think suitable, and he'll find Toby's murderer. Will you also speak to Aubrey? He'll be relieved to know that history hasn't repeated itself."

12

The next morning after breakfast, Freddie went to the Vixen. As he walked along the edge of the garden toward the terrace, he met Aubrey's daughters and Felix, gathered in a little group, and stopped to ask the girls how Evelyn was.

"He's still shut up in his room," Alma reported. "Reg has been trying to convince him to come out, but he won't hear of it."

"He can't hide away forever," said Felix. "I must say I'm disappointed in him. I know he's had a terrible shock, finding his friend Toby dead and having their little secret brought out, but I don't think it's as bad for him as he fears. If he'd only be brave and face up to things, he'd be all right."

"He's waiting for the Marshes to leave. Mellie too." Isolde glanced toward the green where the pavilion had been, where Amelia and Kell were talking together. "They've made it clear what they think of his treatment of her. Dotty told me what Mellie's mother said about it."

"We can't blame them, can we?" said Alma. "Even if he is our brother."

"I'm sorry for Ev," said Felix, "but he's brought much of it on himself. Perhaps it's best that Mellie returns to Marsh Hall with her family. Once she's gone and he gets over poor Toby's death, Evvy might become more like his old self again."

"Are you going to see Ev, Freddie?" asked Isolde.

"I might if Reg will let me, but it was your father I wanted to speak to. Is he in?"

"Father's always in," Alma said with her customary laugh, and gestured toward the partially open door to the study.

When Freddie went up, he found Aubrey seated at his desk and staring at a dyed and embossed leather packet. This packet would normally be rolled into a neat little cylinder, but it was now open and spread flat on the slanted desktop. Freddie could see that there were five narrow sheaths in the inner lining, and in each but one was a small bone-handled knife. Aubrey held the fifth knife, which he'd been using to carve his latest piece. The finished carving stood on the work-table.

Freddie tapped gently on the glass of the door. At the sound, Aubrey turned quickly, startled. "Oh, Freddie, it's you. What is it?" He slipped the knife into the empty sheath with some difficulty; his hand shook.

"I came to tell you," Freddie said as he entered the room, "I've found out who beat Christopher Glovins all those years ago. I've seen them and I don't believe they were involved in Toby's death. Uncle Percy wanted you to know that the two incidents aren't connected."

Aubrey let out a sharp, hysterical bark of laughter. He sounded so like Evelyn had the last time Freddie had seen him that the young man grew alarmed.

"Uncle Aubrey, what's wrong?" He came forward anxiously. "Please, tell me what's happened."

"You're a clever lad, Freddie. You seem to know so much. Do you know about this?" Aubrey waved his hand over the packet of knives spread open before him.

"Know about what?" It took Freddie a moment to understand. "Has one of your knives been taken?" The set was obviously complete. "Oh, I see... one was gone, and now it's been put back." He felt a small chill creep up his spine as the implications of this were borne upon him. Who could have taken it? And why? Was it the one the police were searching for?

"I was surprised to see it returned to its proper place. Very much surprised!" Observing the older man's agitation, Freddie thought that 'shocked' or 'stunned' would be more apt descriptions. "I'm pleased to have it back at last, but I can't help wondering... who do you suppose put it here?"

"I don't know," Freddie answered, "but I can guess." He was considering the possibilities. Who would have the opportunity? An idea was already beginning to form.

"Can you?" Aubrey looked at him in amazement.

"Yes, and I think I can find out if I'm right almost immediately. Will you excuse me please?"

If he was right and the knife that had been returned to Aubrey was the one that had killed Toby, only one of two people could have taken it away from the grove and put it back in the packet. Only two people would have a reason to. Whether one or both were involved in Toby's murder remained to be seen.

When he left Aubrey's study, Freddie went straight upstairs to Evelyn's room. The two were there together, Evelyn and Reginald, the younger sitting on the bed and the elder in a chair beside it. They were in the midst of a heated discussion.

"But I can't face her, Reg. She must hate me."

"Felix told you that she doesn't. At least have the decency to say goodbye to the girl before she goes–"

They stopped when Freddie appeared. He addressed Evelyn first, "All right, Ev, no more lies. Did you take the knife?"

Both brothers stared at him, blankly astonished. "The knife?" squeaked Evelyn. "I didn't do anything with it. Freddie, I swear to you, I never saw it. There was only Toby, lying there, and all that blood..."

"Freddie Babington!" Reginald roared, leaping to his feet. "I told you to leave my brother alone. Uncle Percival says he's innocent, and the police agree. You aren't to badger him." He seized Freddie with his one hand and tried to shove him out of the room. Freddie held his ground and refused to be budged.

"I have to do it, Reg," he said. "I need the truth. If it wasn't Evelyn who took the knife, then it must be you."

Reginald released him. "How- how do you know that?"

"No one else could have," Freddie replied. "You found it in the grove, didn't you? You took it. What did you do with it?"

"I didn't kill him!"

"Then why did you take it?" Freddie persisted. "The truth, Reg. If you aren't responsible for Toby's death, then the truth can only help you and help your brother. Tell me."

"You seem to know already," Reginald said grudgingly. "It's just as you say: When I reached Evvy, I saw the knife lying on the grass near the... ah, body. I picked it up and put it in my coat pocket. I don't think Evvy even noticed. Did you, Ev?"

Evelyn shook his head and stared at his brother. "No. But, Reg, why-?"

"It was one of Father's," Reginald told him, then explained to Freddie, "I recognized it instantly. It's an old one with a bone handle, part of the set Father uses for his wood-work. They have his initials carved on the hilts."

"You don't think it's Father?" Evelyn asked, horrified.

"Oh, no," Reg answered with a wary glance at Freddie. "Certainly not. Father's not stupid enough to leave something that so obviously points to him. Someone left it there to implicate him. I meant to thwart them."

"What did you do with the knife?" Freddie asked again.

"I put it back with the others. Father keeps them in the desk in his study. He came out to meet us on the terrace when I brought Evvy in that night. While he was taking Ev up here to his room, I washed the blood off the knife in the garden room sink and put it back in its place before Felix came in to telephone for the police."

"Neither of you took it from the study in the first place?"

"No!" both brothers cried at once, Reg indignantly, Evelyn with the same horrified tone. "Now, does that satisfy you?" Reginald demanded. "Have you got what you're after, Freddie?"

"Yes, I have. Thank you."

"You won't accuse Father?" asked Evelyn. "He's been terribly upset by all of this, and he didn't even know Toby."

"No," said Freddie. "Your father is quite safe." But he wasn't looking forward to telling Aubrey where his knife had been.

He returned to Aubrey's study, where the older man had put away the packet of knives and was pacing the rug. "Ah, Freddie," he said with an anxious little smile. "You weren't gone very long. You didn't even leave this house."

"No. I didn't need to." Freddie decided to come out with it. "It was as I guessed: Reg told me he was the one who brought your knife back to this room."

"Reg?" Aubrey looked completely baffled. "But how– ah, where did he find it?"

"In that grove in the meadow," Freddie said as gently as he could. "It was lying in the grass near Toby's body."

Aubrey's face went white and his eyes widened in shock. His legs seemed to give beneath him and he sank down quickly into the nearest chair.

"He says he didn't take it from here," Freddie hastened to add. "He told me that he saw it when he found Evelyn, knew it was yours, and hid it to protect you. There's no proof that he's guilty of Toby's murder, Uncle Aubrey. We don't know that it's so."

Aubrey didn't find comfort in this reassurance. He let out a low, agonized moan and clutched his head in his hands.

Freddie could do nothing to console Aubrey and so, at the older man's insistence, left him alone and went back outside.

As he stood blinking in the bright sunlight, he looked around at the others in the garden: Felix and the girls in a laughing little group, Kell smoking a cigarette on the lawn, Amelia wandering the shrubbery. Even Billy, who had followed him to the Vixen and was waiting at the far end of the terrace. Everyone seemed so normal, even happy. They thought that the worst had passed... but Freddie knew that it hadn't begun yet.

The problem of the knife perplexed him. If Reginald was telling the truth, who could have taken it from Aubrey's study? Someone in the household? Could it be one of the girls? A servant? What about Felix? He seemed to spend a lot of time at the Vixen. Freddie had seen that the door to the study was usually left open. Anybody could slip in and out in less than a minute. If Aubrey weren't in, it would be easy to find the packet in his desk and take a knife from it. Days might pass before he noticed that one of the set was missing. After it had been taken, had the thief given it to someone else? Who had carried the knife to the grove? Had this same person killed Toby with it? It was entirely possible that two or three people might be involved. Could it be traced through so many hands? Fingerprints were hopeless at this point.

Kell had come to the foot of the terrace steps and was regarding him with concern. "What is it, Freddie?" he asked. "You look as if you've been struck by lightning."

"I feel as if I have." Freddie took his cousin by the arm and they went to the end of the terrace where Billy stood so they could talk without being overheard.

"What's happened?" Kell asked, "What've you found out?"

"It's the knife that killed Toby. It's one of Uncle Aubrey's." Freddie reported all he had just discovered.

"Do you think Reg is telling the truth?" Kell asked once Freddie had finished.

"I don't know. I'd like to believe him, but it looks bad. Uncle Aubrey seems to believe Reg is responsible. I left him sobbing over it."

"How d'you know Mr. Aubrey doesn't know

more about this knife than he's telling?" Billy wondered. "Maybe he's the one who gave it? It sounds more like he's shocked at seeing it come back to him than it being missing."

"He was shocked at finding it returned," Freddie agreed, "but I'm convinced that he was genuinely confused and grieved to learn that Reg was the person who returned it. I'm sure he didn't give it to his son." He looked around quickly. "Where's Phillip?"

"Having a talk with his father," said Kell. "After all this business with Evelyn and Uncle Aubrey, he wants to make up and have things right between them."

"I don't think we should tell him about this 'til we learn more," Freddie decided.

Kell nodded in agreement. He didn't want Phillip upset.

There was a stir of excitement in the garden as Evelyn emerged from the Vixen. He looked around timidly, past the smiles and encouraging remarks of his sisters and Felix. "Where's Mellie?" he asked them. "I saw her from my window. Is she still here?"

"Right here, Ev." Amelia stepped forward. "You wish to speak to me?"

Faced with the girl he had wronged so publicly, Evelyn became shy and skittish. "You'll be leaving tomorrow?"

"My family is leaving," she confirmed coolly. "They've asked me to go with them. Do you think I should? Is it what *you* want, Evvy? Do you care if I stay or go?"

"Mellie, I–" Evelyn took a step backwards towards the door he'd just emerged from as if he meant to retreat, when Amelia's next words stopped him.

"If you don't care, then I'd better go home right

away. But I won't sit forever at Marsh Hall and spend my life sighing after you, Evelyn Tollarhithe. I'll marry someone else!" She glanced in Freddie's direction. "There's someone who'd marry me tomorrow if I asked him. He's stood by me all through this and been perfectly sweet even when he thought I might've killed that boy. The police have been more kind than you have." She went to the foot of the steps and stood looking up at him. "Is that why you won't see me, Ev? Do you believe I murdered Toby?"

"No!"

"Then it must be the other reason—you've never loved me, and want me to go away." She turned and headed toward Foxgrove.

Evelyn came down the steps from the Vixen's terrace and met Felix at the bottom. There was a quick, whispered conference between the two young men; both glanced at Freddie as well, then Evelyn went after Amelia. He caught up with her, took her arm, and the two began to talk more quietly together. They went into the rose garden.

Kell chuckled. "Aunt Eg would never have approved of that!"

Freddie turned to find Billy standing behind him, regarding him with a quizzical expression. "Would you really marry Miss Amelia? Is that what all that talk of a bigger flat was about?"

"It doesn't matter. I doubt that will happen now," Freddie answered.

"I think she's made a rum choice, when she might've had you." Kell put a hand on his arm. "She hasn't broken your heart, has she, old thing?"

"No," said Freddie. "It's quite all right." He wasn't sure if he was sad at this turn of events or relieved.

Phillip came into the garden and approached his friends. "What did I miss?"

"A terrific scene between Ev and Mellie," Kell reported. "We might see a wedding before we leave here."

"And my investigation's begun again," Freddie added. He tried to think of the best way to tell Phillip why without worrying him on his uncle's behalf. "I've found something that suggests a Tollarhithe is involved in this after all."

Phillip asked anxiously, "It's Uncle Aubrey's knives, isn't it?"

"How do you know about it?" Kell asked in amazement.

"I knew Freddie was going to talk to Uncle Aubrey this morning and he'd see the knives," Phillip explained. "I saw one in Uncle Aubrey's study when I was there talking with him the other day. He'd been carving with it. Is that what you found?" he asked Freddie.

Since Phillip knew this much, he might as well know all. "One was used to kill Toby," Freddie told him. "It was left beside his body that night."

"Is that what you were afraid to tell us?" asked Kell.

Phillip nodded. "I was worried that it might be Uncle Aubrey since you two started talking about why he'd want to be rid of Toby, and who might have a pocket-knife like the one that killed him. Uncle Aubrey's had that set of four sharp, little knives he keeps for woodwork for as long as I can remember."

"Five," Freddie corrected him.

"No," said Phillip, "there's only four."

"There are five knives. I saw them myself not half an hour ago."

"Come on, Phil," Kell said. "You can count that high."

"Yes, I can, and there are only four," Phillip insisted. "I've seen them too, hundreds of times. I used to hide in Uncle Aubrey's study whenever Father was angry with me—and that was a lot of the time! I'd watch him work." Then he conceded, "The set's meant to have five, but one's been missing for ages."

Freddie stared at him. Things began to fall into place.

"You all right, Freddie?" Billy asked, concern for Freddie's well-being driving him out of his sulkiness.

"He has that thunderstruck look again," Kell murmured. "It's important, isn't it, Freddie?"

"Yes, very important," Freddie said slowly, and stepped away from them. "I have to talk to Uncle Aubrey."

"It's not Uncle Aubrey, is it?" Phillip pleaded.

"No," Freddie called back to him, and went into Aubrey's house.

Informed by one of the housemaids that the master of the house had been taken ill and was lying down in his room, Freddie decided not to disturb Aubrey right away. He went to find Reginald instead.

Reginald was in the nursery with his wife and child. He looked angry and frightened at the sight of Freddie returning so soon after their last scene, but Phaedra smiled. "We've heard that Mellie and Ev are talking," she said. "I'm so glad. I hoped they would sort things out between themselves if only Evelyn could be made to behave reasonably."

"I was the one who made him go and speak to her," said Reginald.

"Yes, dear, and a good thing you did," Phaedra responded as if she were talking to her little boy, and turned to give the nursery maid the child to be put down for a nap.

Freddie placed a hand on Reg's arm and spoke softly, "I'd like a word with you, please."

"Oh, for mercy's sake!" Reg huffed in exasperation, but he left the nursery with Freddie. "Aren't you done with us yet?" he hissed once they were alone.

"Nearly done," Freddie assured him. "I have one last question about that knife you found in the grove."

"I told you, I didn't take it from Father's study. I don't know how it got there."

"No, it isn't that. When you put it back in your father's study, you took the packet out of his desk."

"Yes, that's right," Reg said impatiently. "That's where he always keeps it, in the top drawer."

"Did you happen to notice if your father had one knife out for his work?"

"No, I didn't. I didn't want to turn on a light and draw attention to myself. I went straight to the desk—it's under the window, and there was enough light on it for me to see what I was doing. Anyway, I soon saw Father had already put the one he was using back into its place."

Freddie knew Aubrey hadn't done so until this morning. He tried to keep the rising excitement from his voice as he asked, "Then you did see how many of the pockets were empty?"

"Yes, I noticed that," Reginald answered. "There were two empty. But that's perfectly right. One's missing."

"Phillip's told me the same. It's been gone from

the set for as long as he can remember. How long ago was it lost, do you know?"

"As a matter of fact, I don't," Reg snapped. "It's always been missing. Father's had that set of knives since he was a boy. For all I know, he lost it long before I was born. What's all this about, Freddie?"

"I'll explain it later," said Freddie, "when I understand it. Thank you, Reg. I'm sorry I've put you to so much trouble."

Reginald looked confused and somewhat distrustful. "You don't suspect any of us any longer?"

"No," said Freddie. "You needn't worry." He left the Vixen, his head whirling. The clues seemed to point toward one person, one who made the least sense. It was impossible to believe. And yet...

He needed to be alone to think things through. The garden was full of people, so he went into Foxgrove and up to his bedroom. The window was open, and he climbed out to sit on the granite ledge. He wasn't likely to be disturbed here.

Some time passed before Billy found him and peeked out to ask, "Are you all right, Freddie? It's time for lunch."

"I'm not hungry," Freddie replied. "I want to think. Hand me my cigarette case, please? I left it on the mantelpiece."

Billy, who knew better than to bother Freddie when he was in one of his 'thinking' moods, got the cigarette case, handed it out the window, and left Freddie alone.

Nearly an hour later, Freddie climbed back in through the window and came downstairs. He wanted to talk to Sir Percival, but the baronet was among the party just leaving the dining room; before Freddie could draw his uncle's attention, Amelia came forward.

"I wondered where you'd gone," she said as she led him away from the group. "I suppose you know that I made it up with Evelyn."

Freddie acknowledged that he'd guessed this from what he'd witnessed in the garden.

"Ev told me that Uncle Percy and Mr. Thornton suggested he leave the country until this whole awful business is forgotten. He wants to go on a tour of southern France and Italy, just as we'd planned for our honeymoon. I'm going with him. We'll be married after all. Of course, things won't be quite the same," she admitted. "I see now that Ev isn't what I imagined him to be. He's weak. He doesn't know what he wants, and he needs someone to be firm with him." Her eyes flickered over Freddie's face as she added, "Not everyone's pleased for us. Mother seems to think I'm making a mistake—perhaps I am—but she says she hopes we'll be happy."

Freddie repeated this same wish for her happiness. "I hope that Ev knows just how lucky he is. He can't possibly deserve you."

Percival smiled when he noticed Freddie standing alone in the hallway after Amelia had gone. "There you are! We missed you at luncheon. Your manservant said that you had something to think about." As he came closer, Percival lowered his voice and added, "I gather that your investigation is continuing after all?"

"Yes, Uncle. Have you spoken to Mr. Thornton yet?"

"I telephoned this morning. There was some trouble with Tibby Glovins last night. They found that other boy, you know."

"Benny Wegman?" asked Freddie.

"That's right. He was in some sort of accident and died in hospital yesterday afternoon. Your policeman-friend had poor Mrs. Wegman come to identify him. When he heard the news from his father, Tibby went out and got drunk. He was wandering in the small hours after the Boar's Head shut its doors, shouting in the streets at the top of his voice. The local constable took him into custody and Thorton tells me he's still sleeping it off. I thought I'd go this afternoon to see him."

"May I go with you?" Freddie requested. "Uncle Percival, I want to call a few people together: Mr. Thornton, John Deffords if he's here. We may as well meet at the local police station as anywhere else. Can you arrange it? Mr. Glovins should be there too. And we must tell Uncle Aubrey. He mayn't be up to coming with us, but he holds information that will help to clear things up."

"I don't know if I can manage Mr. Glovins, but I'll see to it otherwise." Percival looked extremely interested. "So, Toby's murder is connected with what happened to his father after all,"

"I'm afraid it is," Freddie answered.

"And do you know who killed the boy?"

Freddie nodded. "Yes, I do."

13

They met again half an hour later at the front door of Foxgrove. Freddie found his friends and quickly explained where he was going, and why. Percival went to the Vixen and returned with Aubrey, who looked very pale but determined.

"I'm going with you," he announced. "I want to. Pal's told me that you know who the murderer is,

Freddie."

"I believe so," Freddie answered. "You knew it too this morning, didn't you?"

Aubrey nodded solemnly. "Yes, but I don't understand why. Do you?"

"I've an idea, but I'd rather wait 'til we're in the company of the police to discuss it."

Sir Percival looked from one to the other. "I don't know what you're talking about. I don't know who it is, and I wish you'd tell me."

Freddie spoke a name.

"Oh, no." Percival made a small sound of surprise and disbelief, and laid a hand on Aubrey's arm. "If an arrest is made, this can't be handled privately, Aubrey."

"Yes, I know," Aubrey acknowledged. "I'll have to explain it to Evelyn and the other children, but they'll learn the truth one way or another. It's better if they hear it from me."

The chauffeur brought the baronet's automobile around from the garage; all three got in and rode in silence to the Foxborough police station on the far side of the town. When they arrived, Christopher Glovins was already there with his daughter, pleading with Thornton for Tibby's release.

"The lad's come to no harm," Thornton was trying to reassure them. "He was raising riot last night, shouting threats against–" he stopped when his more prestigious visitors entered and quickly amended what he'd been about to say, "against people he shouldn't. We can't allow that. I know he's lost his brother, but that's no excuse for his behavior. Since the lad put up a fight when the constable on duty tried to quiet him, we had no choice but to bring him in."

"Where is he?" asked Torie. "What've you done

with him?"

"He's in the cell, Miss Glovins. When the constable last looked in on him, he was still asleep. You can take him home when he wakes, if he's willing to behave himself."

"It'd help if we saw some justice for our Toby," said Torie. "Have you found out who killed him yet?" She glared at Freddie accusingly. "Have you, Mr. Babington?"

"As a matter of fact, that's just what we've come for," said Percival. "To see justice done for your brother."

Aubrey was watching Christopher Glovins. "Hello, Toffer," he said quietly. "It's been a very long time. I'm sorry we couldn't meet again under happier circumstances."

Freddie realized that this was the first time Mr. Glovins and Aubrey had seen each other in more than thirty years. He tried to imagine them as they were the last time they'd met. Had they been very like their sons before Aubrey had had the spirit crushed out of him and turned within himself, and before Christopher Glovins had nursed his hatred of the Tollarhithe family past all reason? Had any of that old emotion survived, or had too many years passed and too much come between them? But it was useless to think of that now.

Torie, although somewhat intimidated by Sir Percival's presence, still looked resentful. Mr. Glovins, however, only seemed abashed; he wouldn't meet Aubrey's eyes. "We ought to be leaving," he said, and tried to skirt the Tollarhithes to reach the exit. "Torie, come along. These gentlemen have business with Mr. Thornton. They'll want to speak to him without us here. We'll come back for Tibby when he wakes up."

"No, please, don't go," Percival insisted. "We wanted you to join us. It'll save the trouble of a journey to the butcher's shop if you remain."

"We're waiting for one more person to join us." Freddie asked Thornton, "You've phoned Inspector Deffords?"

"Yes, and he's on his way."

But Mr. Glovins didn't want to wait. He was anxious to leave, until Freddie said, "Stay, please. You'll want to hear what I have to say. I'm going to tell the police who's responsible for Toby's death."

Mr. Glovins turned to regard Freddie with wide, almost blank eyes. "You know?"

"I know almost everything that happened that night," Freddie replied quietly.

At these words, Mr. Glovins crumpled as if he'd been struck. His daughter caught him by the arm, and he sank into a chair that Thornton hastily provided for him.

Mr. Glovins looked up at his daughter. "Torie," he said, "I must stay, but I want you to go home. You mustn't be here."

"No, Dad, I want to stay. If Mr. Babington knows who killed Toby, then I want to hear it." She whirled to Freddie. "Tell us who it is!"

"It's rather a long and complicated story," Freddie said. He was reluctant to speak in front of this young girl, but if she refused to go at her father's request, she surely wouldn't leave at his. She'd hear the truth very soon, in any case.

"Well, I'm interested in hearing it," said Mr. Thornton, with the air of a man looking forward to a good tale. He escorted the group into an empty interview room behind the front desk and showed them all to seats before taking a chair for himself. Torie remained standing beside her father's chair; Christopher Glovins held the girl by wrapping one arm around her waist.

While they were seating themselves, Deffords arrived. Freddie went to the station entrance to meet him. "I hear you're going to name the murderer," the inspector said, then glanced through the open doorway at the group gathered in the room beyond. "Suspects in the drawing room, is it?"

"It's no drawing room, but it must do under the circumstances. The Glovinses would hardly be willing to come to Foxgrove. You've already got the prime suspect, John, whom I'm afraid is past being arrested," Freddie told him softly.

"You mean the Wegman boy." Deffords didn't sound as if he were surprised.

"Yes. Whether or not you'll want to make other arrests after you hear what I have to say will be up to you and the Deputy Chief Constable."

They went in.

"I'd like to request a certain amount of leniency regarding some of the actions in the story I'm about to tell you," Freddie began, addressing the two police officials. "Crimes, if any were committed, occurred a very long time ago—or if they were more recent, were done out of a desire to protect loved ones. What we're all most interested in here is solving Toby Glovins's murder—I think we can agree on that. To understand how this murder came about, we must go back to a similar incident that happened here in Foxborough more than thirty years ago. Sir Alvin, the last baronet, his brother Rupert, and another member of the Tollarhithe family hired a pair of farm-laborers to beat a young boy." Mr. Glovins flinched as Freddie said this, and Torie bent her head over his to murmur something comforting. "They thought he'd gotten above himself by becoming friends with one of their sons."

"Because they were friends?" Thornton said incredulously, and then understanding dawned.

Freddie didn't say more about the identity of these boys, but Deffords glanced from Mr. Glovins to Sir Percival, then to Aubrey, since the baronet's cousin had no other reason for being there. Torie followed his gaze and began to regard Aubrey with curiosity.

Thornton kept his eyes on Mr. Glovins as he spoke to Freddie. "As you say, it happened years ago, but what has it to do with Toby's murder? Are you suggesting that the same sort of thing's occurred again?"

"That was what I feared when I engaged Freddie to look into this," Sir Percival said.

"I found that it wasn't so," Freddie added, "but this morning I came upon an important piece of evidence that showed me the truth. It has to do with a certain knife."

Deffords was alert. "The murder weapon? Have you found it?"

"I can describe it for you. When we began this investigation, my cousin Kell said that there are so many pocket knives and pen knives about, anybody might have one like it. But that's not so. The knife that killed Toby was quite distinctive. It's a fine craftsman's knife, bone-handled, with the initials 'AT' carved into the hilt. It was one of a set given as a gift to Aubrey Tollarhithe as a boy. All the Tollarhithe family is familiar with them."

"Does he have it now?" Thornton looked expectantly at Aubrey.

Aubrey produced the knife from the pocket of his tweed coat. "I'm afraid it's practically useless as evidence," he said apologetically as he handed it hilt-first to Thornton. "It's been cleaned."

"Did you clean it, Mr. Tollarhithe?" asked Deffords, and when Aubrey shook his head, continued, "Did you carry it away from the grove on the night of the murder?"

"No. I was never near the meadow that night."

"Then who took it and washed it?" Thornton wanted to know.

"Reginald did," Freddie answered. "Evelyn's elder brother. He told me so himself this morning."

Torie's eyes flashed. "Did he kill Toby?"

"No," Freddie assured her. "He found the knife beside Toby's body. He knew at once that it belonged to his father and carried it away with him when he escorted Evelyn back to the Vixen's Den. He washed it and put it back with the others in his father's desk, where he thought it had come from. But he was mistaken. This particular knife hadn't sat alongside its fellows for a very long time." He turned to Aubrey. "Uncle Aubrey, when you showed me that set of knives this morning, you said you were glad to have the missing one back 'at last'? How long had it been gone?"

"More than thirty years."

"That was the one Reg returned? You're quite sure?"

"Absolutely. They aren't identical. There are slight differences between one blade and the next. I know them all well."

"But the missing one wasn't lost, was it? You gave it away as a present to a friend."

Aubrey nodded.

"Is that why you wept when I told you where Reg had found it?" Freddie asked. "I thought at the time that you believed Reg was guilty of Toby's murder, but that wasn't it at all. You'd realized what had happened. I didn't understand, not 'til I learned from Phillip and Reg that one knife had been missing for longer than either of them can remember. Then I recalled that Miss Glovins told us her father had a knife that belonged to one of the Tollarhithes. You gave it to Mr. Glovins when you were boys and he kept it all those years." Freddie turned to Christopher Glovins, who sat very still. "Who did you give it to, Mr. Glovins? To Benny before you sent him off to the grove?"

"No," Mr. Glovins answered after a long silence. "I gave it to my Toby, weeks ago. I wanted to remind him what a pledge of friendship meant to a Tollarhithe."

"You certainly didn't intend for your own son to be killed," said Freddie. "Was it Evelyn you were after?"

"No!" Mr. Glovins protested. "I didn't mean for anybody to die. Toby came home the night before. He'd just talked with Evelyn Tollarhithe. He was angry and looking for revenge. He said he was going to spoil the wedding, but I said we could do something better. I had him write to young Evelyn, asking him to come to their meeting spot once more, but Benny would be waiting there instead of Toby and give the lad a good thumping, rough 'm up a bit, to pay back all the Tollarhithes for what they did to us. Benny'd do whatever I said. He was that grateful to me for keeping him on."

Aubrey had been regarding his old friend with great sympathy and pity until he heard this plan.

"Evelyn doesn't know a thing about that! He doesn't deserve a beating any more than you did. How could you think of punishing my son for it?"

Christopher looked up at last to meet Aubrey's eyes. "My boy's paid for it worse. He's dead, same as if I'd stabbed him myself!" he wailed in an agony of grief. He let go of Torie, who drew away from him, whispering, "No...oh, no," in disbelief.

"How did your son come to be there?" Deffords asked him quietly.

"I told him to stay home." Tears flowed down the butcher's face. "I've done nothing but turn it over in my mind since we had the news. I sit beside him, laid out in the parlor, night and day, thinking how it happened. Poor Toby must've gone to warn Evelyn. Maybe he tried to push Benny off home and Benny wouldn't go. Or maybe, among the trees, Benny mistook my lad for the other and set upon him." He shook his head. "If they were struggling, Toby must've stabbed himself, accidentally. He was the one that had the knife, not Benny."

"That would explain the odd angle of the wound," murmured Thornton. "The doctor said it might be self-inflicted. Would Benny have tried to take the knife from him in a struggle?"

Mr. Glovins shook his head. "No, Benny wouldn't've hurt Toby, not deliberately."

"But he ran off afterwards."

"I expect that once Toby was dead, Benny got frightened. He knew he couldn't come back to me nor go to his mother. He wasn't too bright, so all he could think to do was get away as fast as he could and keep running. He's dead now, too, and it's all my fault." Mr. Glovins looked up at Thornton and said, "You must do as you will. I don't care now, except for..."

He turned in his seat to find his stunned daughter leaning against the wall behind him and moaning, "No, Dad. No, it can't be true. Say it isn't."

"I'm sorry, lass, but it is. I didn't want you to hear. Will you do one thing for me? When your brother wakes, you must be the one to tell him. He won't believe it if the police or one of the Tollarhithes tells him."

"I think he's guessed the truth already," said Freddie. "Unless I'm mistaken, the news of Benny's death was what sent him off on last night's tear."

"What will happen to Mr. Glovins?" Freddie asked Sir Percival as they returned to Foxgrove. "Will he be arrested?"

"It's up to the police to determine if charges will be brought against him. If he hadn't sought revenge against a young man who had nothing to do with it, I would pity him."

"It's that poor, dead boy I feel most sorry for," said Aubrey. "In spite of his father's efforts to poison his mind, he couldn't sit by in the end and allow Evelyn to be brutally beaten. He'd still be alive if he hadn't tried to intervene."

"What will happen to the younger brother and sister?" asked Freddie. "Will they be all right? This has been an incredible shock to them, and they shouldn't be left by themselves at such a time."

"They won't be," Percival promised. "They have relatives in Foxborough who will take them in until they know how things are settled with their father. No matter how it turns out, I'll look after them. They won't like it, but I rather feel that they're my responsibility. I can't forget that this began with our family."

The wedding of Amelia Marsh and Evelyn Tollarhithe was a more quiet affair than originally planned, since most of the guests had gone home. There was also a measure of sadness in the ceremony, for Toby Glovins's funeral service would be held at St. Barnabas later that same day. But Amelia wore her dress festooned with froths of old lace and looked very pretty, and the bride's and groom's immediate families were there to see the two wed and then to see them off on their delayed honeymoon. Since no party followed the morning ceremony, only an old-fashioned breakfast, the newlyweds were ready to leave by noon.

After she'd made her farewells to her mother, aunts, and cousins, Amelia took Freddie's hand. "I'm sorry Freddie, if I disappointed you."

"You haven't been a disappointment, Mellie," Freddie replied. "I hope you'll have everything you wished for."

She smiled. "I wouldn't have it at all if it weren't for you." She gave him a kiss on the cheek before climbing into the auto beside her new husband, who looked a little jealous.

Once the young couple had gone, the last of the guests also prepared to be on their way. But there were a few matters Freddie had to see to before he and his friends could depart.

He had to talk to Aunt Emily. Since she'd been the first to ask him to look into this murder, he thought she ought to hear how his investigation had concluded.

"How very sad," the lady said when she learned the history of Aubrey and Christopher Glovins. "No. It's more than sad—it's quite tragic. I remember them as boys. I never knew 'til now how their friendship was broken up. To think there's been so much unhappiness because of it, even to this day." She went to say goodbye to her son before joining Matilda and Theresa to return to Marsh Hall.

Sir Percival went into Foxborough that afternoon; when he returned, Freddie met with him in his study one last time while Billy was upstairs packing. Percival was at his desk, studying the faded writing in a large, old, dusty-looking book.

"I've seen Mr. Thornton," he told Freddie. "You'll be pleased to hear that he's released Mr. Glovins. He also told me something I think you'll be interested in: an aged local farmer named Enoch Twigg has left his home."

"Left?" Freddie echoed, surprised.

"His family doesn't know where he's gone but there's every sign that he left of his own accord. He packed a bag and left the night before last." He watched Freddie carefully as he delivered this information. "The name of Twigg sounded familiar to me, so I've looked it up in my father's old estate journal." Sir Percival nodded to indicate the book on his desk. "It seems that my father granted Enoch Twigg and his brother a farm as a freehold about thirty years ago. He didn't note why he chose to make such a generous gift, but I can guess. I expect Mr. Twigg's gone for good. Perhaps that's best."

"Perhaps it is," Freddie agreed. He could imagine the panic that had prompted the old man's flight.

"So that's that. It's been a pleasure to work with you, Freddie." Percival went with Freddie to the study door and offered to shake his hand. "You've grown up to be an exceptional young man. This has been an ugly business from beginning to end and you got to the heart of it. Emily didn't exaggerate in her estimation of your abilities, and Phillip hasn't gone wrong by being a friend of yours."

"Thank you," Freddie answered modestly, but he was touched and gratified by this praise.

After he made his farewells to Lady Egeria, he found Kell and Billy waiting in the front hall with their bags. "Phil's not ready yet," Kell reported.

Phillip joined them a few minutes later, with no luggage.

"Haven't you packed?" Kell asked him. "We'll be leaving soon."

"I won't be," Phillip said. "You know you can't cram four people into that little roadster of yours, and besides..." he looked around at the others and announced, "I've decided to stay on and settle some things with my parents. Father and I– we have a lot to talk about. And Mother and Auntie Di mean to settle 'the problem' of my engagement. So do I. In my own way, of course."

Kell grinned. "Do you want me to stay with you?" he offered.

"If you don't mind, I'd rather you didn't," Phillip answered almost apologetically. "I think I'd better do this by myself. I'm at my best, you know, when I have to stand on my own. I'll come up to London for a day or two before I have to be back at Cambridge."

After Phillip returned to the house, the other three loaded their bags into the roadster and drove down the avenue to the park's front gate. Just beyond the gate lay the churchyard of St. Barnabas and they could see that Toby's funeral service was in progress. A small party was gathered around the open grave: Mr. Glovins and his two surviving children, a pair of elderly women whom Freddie guessed were the relatives Sir Percival had spoken of, a few other neighbors, and the same vicar who had performed the wedding ceremony that morning. Not among this group, but at the lych-gate, stood Inspector Deffords.

Freddie urged Kell to stop. "I thought you'd gone."

Deffords shook his head. "My work here wasn't finished."

"Oh, I say," Freddie glanced at the party in the churchyard, "you're not going to arrest Mr. Glovins after all?"

"No. Mr. Thornton decided against it. Sir Percival and Aubrey Tollarhithe might want to charge him with the assault intended on Evelyn, but I don't think they will. That didn't come off and Evelyn wasn't harmed. He didn't even lose Miss Marsh over it." Deffords looked as if he were ready to offer sympathy if Freddie needed it. "Mr. Glovins didn't intend the deaths of the other two young men. Toby's death was by misadventure and Benny Wegman's was an accident."

"Are you quite sure?"

"I questioned the lorry driver who struck Benny. He said that the boy darted straight into the road in front of him without looking and he wasn't able to stop in time. I've heard what Benny had to say too."

Freddie was surprised. "I didn't realize you'd spoken to him before he died."

"I didn't. I got it second-hand from the lorry driver and a hospital nurse who looked after him. Both said that he kept repeating 'I'm sorry' and 'I didn't mean it' or 'I didn't mean to do it.' The nurse also said that he spoke of being pulled about by someone, putting up a fight, and being frightened by the sight of a knife. They didn't know what he was talking about, but I think we can both guess. Toby must've done all he could to try and drive Benny away before Evelyn arrived."

"You knew that much yesterday, before we met at the police station?"

"There was no chance to tell you. Besides, I had no idea what Benny was doing in the meadow. I hadn't yet heard about the part Mr. Glovins played in his son's death. That was all your work and I wouldn't have missed seeing you put it all together."

"Have you told Mrs. Wegman?"

"That's why I came back today. She already heard some of what happened with her son and Toby Glovins, but she had to know that he wasn't a murderer. A simple-minded brute, perhaps, but not a cold-blooded killer. That's got to be some comfort."

Kell and Billy in the roadster were beginning to look impatient.

"I must go," said Freddie. "It was a pleasure working with you again, John. If there another murder brings us together one day, I do hope that, next time, none of my relatives will be involved."

"So do I," said the inspector. "And there will be a next time."

Kathryn L. Ramage has a B.A. and M.A. in English lit and has been writing for as long as she can remember. She lives in Maryland with three cats. As well as being the author of numerous short stories, novellas, and essays, she is the author of "Maiden in Light," "The Wizard's Son," and "Sonnedragon," novels set on an alternate Earth whose history has diverged from ours somewhere during the medieval period. All three are part of an intended series of fantasy novels that mostly take place in a dukedom called the Northlands, a part of the Norman Empire that roughly covers the north-eastern U.S. For more information, please visit her website at www.klr.wapshottpress.com

Also by Kathryn L. Ramage

The Wizard's Son

Maiden in Light

Sonnedragon

Storylandia 10: Death Among the Marshes

Storylandia 16: The Abrupt Disappearance of Cousin Wilfrid

Thank you to the Wapshott Press sponsors, supporters, and Friends of the Wapshott Press.

Muna Deriane

Ann Siemens

Suzanne Siegel

Debbie Jones

Steven Acker

Jennifer Bentson

Kathleen Bonagofsky

Carol Colin

Ted Waltz

Cynthia Henderson

Aubrey Hicks

Nancy Lilly

Jeff Morawetz

Patricia Nerad

Amanda Nerad

Elaine Padilla

Bradley Rader

Kathleen M. Warner

The Wapshott Press is a 501(c)(3) not-for-profit enterprise publishing work by emerging and established authors and artists. We publish books that should be published. We are very grateful to the people who believe in our plans and goals, as well as our hopes and dreams. Please visit our website at www.WapshottPress.org to learn more about us.

www.ingramcontent.com/pod-product-compliance
Lightning Source LLC
Chambersburg PA
CBHW070924130626
46555CB00001B/266